PENGUIN BOOKS

JUMP AND OTHER STORIES

Nadine Gordimer was born and lives in South Africa. Her collections of short stories include *Friday's Footprint*, *Livingstone's Companions*, *No Place Like: Selected Stories*, *A Soldier's Embrace*, *Something Out There* and *Why Haven't You Written?* Among her novels are *A World of Strangers*, *A Guest of Honour*, *The Conservationist*, joint winner of the Booker Prize, *The Late Bourgeois World*, *Burger's Daughter*, *July's People*, *A Sport of Nature* and *My Son's Story*, all published by Penguin. She has also collaborated with the photographer David Goldblatt on two books, *On the Mines* and *Lifetimes: Under Apartheid*, and has published a collection of essays, *The Essential Gesture*. She has received numerous literary awards, including the Malaparte Prize from Italy, the Nelly Sachs Prize from Germany, the Scottish Arts Council's Neil Gunn Fellowship, the French International award, the Grand Aigle d'Or and the Benson Medal from the Royal Society of Literature.

NADINE GORDIMER

JUMP
AND OTHER STORIES

PENGUIN BOOKS

PENGUIN BOOKS

Published by the Penguin Group
Penguin Books Ltd, 27 Wrights Lane, London W8 5TZ, England
Penguin Books USA Inc., 375 Hudson Street, New York, New York 10014, USA
Penguin Books Australia Ltd, Ringwood, Victoria, Australia
Penguin Books Canada Ltd, 10 Alcorn Avenue, Toronto, Ontario, Canada M4V 3B2
Penguin Books (NZ) Ltd, 182–190 Wairau Road, Auckland 10, New Zealand

Penguin Books Ltd, Registered Offices: Harmondsworth, Middlesex, England

First published in Great Britain by Bloomsbury 1991
Published in Penguin Books 1992
1 3 5 7 9 10 8 6 4 2

The publishers wish to thank the magazines in which the stories first appeared, some in
slightly different form: "Jump" and "The Moment Before the Gun Went Off" in
Harper's; "Comrades" in *Interview*; "The Ultimate Safari", "Some Are Born to Sweet
Delight", "Spoils" and "What Were You Dreaming?" in *Granta*; "Teraloyna" in the
Boston Globe; "My Father Leaves Home", "Home" and "Amnesty" in the *New Yorker*;
"A Find" and "Once Upon a Time" in *Salmagundi*; "A Journey" in *Playboy*; "Keeping
Fit" in *Mirabella*; and "Safe Houses" in *Grand Street*

Printed in England by Clays Ltd, St Ives plc

For Pascale and Paule Taramasco

and Katherine Cassirer

CONTENTS

Jump

He is aware of himself in the room, behind the apartment door, at the end of a corridor, within the spaces of this destination that has the name HOTEL LEBUVU in gilt mosaic where he was brought in. The vast lobby where a plastic-upholstered sofa and matching easy chairs are stranded, the waiting elevator in its shaft that goes up floor after floor past empty halls, gleaming signs—CONFERENCE CENTRE, TROPICANA BUFFET, THE MERMAID BAR—he is aware of being finally reached within all this as in a film a series of dissolves passes the camera through walls to find a single figure, the hero, the criminal. Himself.

The curtains are open upon the dark, at night. When he gets up in the morning he closes them. By now they are on fire with the sun. The day pressing to enter. But his back is turned; he is an echo in the chamber of what was once the hotel.

The chair faces the wide-screen television set they must have installed when they decided where to put him. There is nothing to match its expensive finish—the small deal table and four chairs with hard red plastic-covered seats, the hairy two-division sofa, the Formica-topped stool, the burning curtains whose circles and blotches of pattern dazzle like the flicker of flames: these would be standard for a clientele of transients who spend a night, spill beer, and put out cigarettes under a heel. The silvery convex of the TV screen reflects a dim, ballooned vision of a face, pale and full. He forgets, and passes a hand over cheek and chin, but there is no beard there—it's real that he shaved it off. And they gave him money to fit himself out with the clothes he wears now. The beard (it was dark and vigorous, unlike the fine hair of his head) and the camouflage fatigues tucked into boots that struck authoritatively with each step, the leather-bound beret; took them all off, divested himself of them. There! He must be believed, he was believed. The face pale and sloping away into the pale flesh of the chin: his hidden self produced for them. It's there on the dead screen when he looks up.

They supplied a cassette player of good quality as well as the wide-screen television set. He is playing, so loudly it fills the room, presses counter to the day pressing against the curtains, the music track from a film about an American soldier who becomes brutalized by the atrocities he is forced to commit in Vietnam. He saw the film long ago, doesn't remember it well, and does not visualize its images. He is not listening: the swell and clash, the tympani of conflict, the brass of glory, the chords of thrilling resolve, the maudlin strings of regret, the pauses of disgust—they come from inside him. They flow from him and he sits on and does not meet the image smeared on the screen. Now and then he sees his hand. It never matched the beard, the fatigues, the beret, the orders it signed. It is a slim, white, hairless hand, almost transparent over fragile bones, as the skeleton of a gecko can be seen within its ghostly skin. The knuckles are delicately pink—clean, clean hand, scrubbed and scrubbed—but along the V between first and second fingers there is the shit-coloured stain of nicotine where the cigarette burns down. They were prepared to spend foreign currency on him. They still supply from somewhere the imported brand he prefers; packets are stacked up amply in their cellophane, within reach. And he can dial room service as indicated on the telephone that stands on the floor, and, after a long wait, someone will come and bring cold beer. He was offered whisky, anything he liked, at the beginning, and he ordered it although he had never been one to drink spirits, had made the choice, in his profession, of commanding the respect accorded the superiorly disciplined personality rather than the kind admiringly given to the hard-living swaggerer. The whisky has stopped coming; when he orders a bottle nothing is said but it is not delivered.

As if it mattered.

Covered by the volume of the music, there is the silence. Nothing said about the house: the deal included a house, he was given to understand it would be one of the fine ones left behind and expropriated by the State in the name of the people, when the colonials fled. A house with a garden and watchman for privacy, security (in his circumstances), one of the houses he used to ride past when he was the schoolboy son of a civil servant living here in a less affluent white quarter. A house and a car. Eventually some sort of decent position. Rehabilitated. He had thought of information, public relations (with his international experience); it was too soon to say, but they didn't say no.

Everything he wanted: that was to be his reward. The television crews came—not merely the tin-pot African ones but the BBC, CBS, Antenne 2, Zweites Deutsches Fernsehen—and the foreign correspondents flew in with their tape recorders. He was produced at press conferences in the company of the Commander of the Armed Forces, the Minister of Defence, and their aides elegant as the overthrown colonial ones had been. A flower arrangement among the water carafes. Him displayed in his provided clothes, his thighs that had been imposing in fatigues too fleshy when crossed in slightly shiny tropical trousers, his chin white, soft and naked where the beard was gone, his hair barbered neat and flat with the dun fringe above the forehead, clippers run up the nape—on his big hunched body he saw in the newspaper photographs the head of a little boy with round bewildered eyes under brows drawn together and raised. He told his story. For the first few months he told his story again and again, in performance. Everyone has heard it, now. On the table with the four chairs drawn up a cold fried egg waits on a plate covered by another plate. A jug of hot water has grown tepid beside a tin of instant coffee. Someone has brought these things and gone away. Everyone has gone away. The soaring, billowing music in the room is the accompaniment the performance never had. When the tape has ended he depresses the rewind button to play it again.

They never mention the house or the car and he doesn't know how to bring up the subject—they hardly ever come to see him any more, but maybe that's natural because the debriefing is over, they're satisfied. There's nothing more to tell the television crews and the press. There's nothing more he can think of—think back! think back!—to find to say. They've heard about his childhood in this capital, this country to which he has been returned. That he was an ordinary colonial child of parents who'd come out from Europe to find a better life where it was warm and there were opportunities. That it was warm and there was the sea and tropical fruit, blacks to dig and haul, but the opportunity was nothing grander than the assured tenure of a white man in the lower ranks of the civil service. His parents were not interested in politics, never. They were not interested in the blacks. They didn't think the blacks would ever affect their lives and his. When the colonial war began it was away in the North; troops came from the 'mother' country to deal with it. The boy would perhaps become an accountant, certainly something one rung above his father, because each generation must better itself, as they had done by emigrating. He grew up taking for granted the activities and outlets for adventurous play that had no place in the reality of the blacks' lives, the blacks' war: as an adolescent he bonded with his peers through joining the parachute club, and he jumped—the rite of passage into manhood.

In the capital, the revolution was achieved overnight by a relinquishment of power by Europe, exacted by the indigenous people through years of war in the rural areas. A few statues toppled in the capital's square and some shops were looted in revenge for exploitation. His parents judged their security by the uninterrupted continuance, at first, of the things that mattered to them: the garbage continued to be collected twice a week and there was fish in the market. Their modest lives would surely not be touched by black rule. He was apprenticed as draughtsman to an architect by then (more prestigious than accountancy) and his week-end hobby, in addition to jumping from the sky, was photography. He even made a bit of pocket money by selling amusing shots of animals and birds to a local paper. Then came the event that—all at once, reeled up as the tape is filling its left cylinder on rewind—the experience that explained everything he had ever done since, everything that he was to confess to, everything he was to inculpate himself for and judge himself on in his performance for the journalists under the monitoring approval of the Commander of the Armed Forces and the Minister of Defence, during the probing of debriefing, the Q and A interviews; and to himself, in fiery dimness behind the curtains' embers, facing the fish-eye of the TV screen, surrounded by the music, alone. He took a photograph of a sea-bird alighting on some sort of tower structure. Soldiers lumbered with sawn-off machine guns seized him, smashed his camera and took him to the police. He was detained for five weeks in a dirty cell the colonial regime had used for blacks. His parents were told he was an imperialist spy—their innocent boy only two years out of school! Of course, this was all in the confusion of the first days of freedom (he would explain to his audience), it was to be expected. And who was that boy to think he could photograph anything he liked, a military installation of interest to the new State's enemies? That white boy.

At this point in the telling came the confession that for the first time in his life he thought about blacks—and hated them. They had smashed his camera and locked him up like a black and he hated them and their government and everything they might do, whether it was good or bad. No—he had not then believed they could ever do anything good for the country where he was born. He was sought out by or he sought out—he was never made to be clear on this small point—white people to whom his parents had successfully appealed to get him released. They soothed him with their indignation over what had happened to him and gave him a substitute for the comradeship of the parachute club (closed down by the blacks' military security) in their secret organization to restore white rule through compliant black proxies. How it was to be done was not yet formulated, allies from neighbouring cold and hot wars had not yet been found, money from international interests wanting access to oil and mineral finds had not been supplied, sources for matériel and mercenaries to put together a rebel army in the bush were still to be investigated. He bent quietly over his drawing board and at night he went to clandestine meetings. He felt importantly patriotic; something new, because his parents had abandoned their country, and this country in which he was born had been taken back by the blacks for themselves. His parents thanked God he was safe in good company, white like them but well off and knowledgeable about how to go on living here where it was warm, trusted to advise one if it were to be time to leave. They were proud when told their son was being sent to Europe to study; an act of philanthropy by compatriots of the country they had all once emigrated from.

Of humble beginnings, he had come into the patrimony of counter-revolution.

The telephone is not only good for house calls that summon the old black man shrunken in khaki who brings the beer, brought the egg and covered it with a second plate.

He can phone long distance every day, if he wants to. There is never a bill; they pay. That was the condition understood—they would provide everything. So he phones his mother every third day in the European city to which she and his father returned when the people who knew about these things said it was time to go. He has only to dial, and it's winter there now and the phone will ring on its crocheted mat in the living-room behind double-glazing, discovered to him (so that was where his parents came from!) when he was set up in the same European city. They must have realized soon that he was not studying. At least not in the sense they would understand, of attending an institute and qualifying for a profession you could name. But it was obvious to them he was doing well, he was highly-thought-of by the people who had recognized the young man's qualities and taken him up after the terrible time when those blacks threw him in prison back where everything was lost, now— the civil servant's pension, the mangoes and passion fruit, the sun. He was involved in the affairs of those people of substance, international business too complicated for him to explain. And confidential. They respected that. A mother and father must never make any move that might jeopardize the opportunities they themselves have not been able to provide. He was always on his way to or from the airport— France, Germany, Switzerland, and other destinations he did not specify. Of course his gift for languages must have been invaluable to the people he worked with rather than for—that was clearly his status. He had not an apartment but a whole house purchased for him in the privacy of one of the best quarters, and his study or office there was not only lined with documents and books but equipped with the latest forms of telecommunication. Foreign associates came to stay; he had a full-time maid. His delicate, ado-lescent's chin disappeared in the soft flesh of good living, and then he grew the beard that came out dark and vigorous giving him the aspect of a man of power. They never saw him wearing the rest of its attributes: the bulky fatigues and the boots and the beret. He visited them in civilian clothes that had come to be his disguise.

The first time he ever used the phone on the floor was when he phoned her, his mother, to tell her he was alive and here. *Where?* How could she ever have supposed it— back, back in this country! The sun, the mangoes (that day there was fruit supplied on the table where the egg congeals, now), the prison a young boy had been thrown into like any black. She wept because she and his father had thought he was dead. He had disappeared two months previously. Without a word; that was one of the conditions he adhered to on his side, he couldn't tell his parents this was not a business trip from which he would return: he was giving up the house, the maid, the first-class air tickets, the im-portant visitors, the book-lined room with the telecom-munications system by which was planned the blowing up of trains, the mining of roads, and the massacre of sleeping villagers back there where he was born.

It is the day to phone her. It's more and more difficult to keep up the obligation. There's nothing left to tell her, either. From weeping gratitude that he was alive, as time has gone by she has come to ask why *she* should be punished in this way, why he should have got mixed up in something that ended so badly.

Over the phone she says, Are you all right?

He asks after his father's health. Does it look like being a mild winter?

Already the wind from the mountains has brought a touch of rheumatism.

Do you need anything? (Money is provided for him to send to his parents, deprived of their pension; that's part of the deal.)

Then there's nothing to say. She doesn't ask if he's suffering from the heat back there, although the sun banks up its fire in the closed curtains, although she knows well enough what the climate's like in summer, and he was gone seven years and cannot reacclimatize. She doesn't want to mention the heat because that is to admit he is back there, she and his father will never understand what it was all about, his life; why he got himself into the fine house, the telecommunications system, the international connections, or why he gave it all up. She says little, in a listless voice, over the phone. But she writes. They deliver her letters, pushed under the door. *Why does God punish me? What have your father and I done? It all started long ago. We were too soft with you. With that parachute nonsense. We should never have allowed it. Giving in, letting you run wild with those boys. It started to go wrong then, we should have seen you were going to make a mess of our lives, I don't know why. You had to go jumping from up there. Do you know what I felt, seeing you fall like that, enjoying yourself frightening us to death while you fooled around with killing yourself? We should have known it. Where it would end. Why did you have to be like that? Why? Why?*

First in the weeks of debriefing and then in the press conferences, he had to say.

They demanded again and again. It was their right.

How could you associate yourself with the murderous horde that burns down hospitals, cuts off the ears of villagers, blows up trains full of innocent workers going home to their huts, rapes children and forces women at gunpoint to kill their husbands and eat their flesh?

He sat there before them sane, and was confronted by the madness. As he sits in the red gloom in front of the wide-screen television set, the fuse of a cigarette between the fingers of his fine white hand and his pale blue eyes clear under puppy-like brows. Shuddering; they couldn't see it but he shuddered within every time to hear listed by them what he knew had happened. How could they come out with it, just like that?

Because horror comes slowly. It takes weeks and months, trickling, growing, mounting, rolling, swelling from the faxed codes of operation, the triumph of arms deals secretly concluded with countries who publicly condemn such transactions; from the word 'destabilization' with its image of some faulty piece of mechanism to be rocked from its base so that a sound structure may be put in its place. He sent the fax, he took the flights to campaign for support from multinational companies interested in access to the oil and minerals the blacks were giving to their rivals, he canvassed Foreign Offices interested in that other term, spheres of influence.

In the fine house where an antique clock played an air over the sudden stutterings of communications installations, the war was intelligence, the miracle of receiving the voice of a general thousands of kilometres away, on the other continent, down there in the bush. When he travelled on his European missions he himself was that fighting man: the beard, the fatigues, the beret. The people he visited saw him as straight from the universal battlefield of Right and Left; the accoutrements transformed him for himself, so it seemed he was emerged from that generic destiny known as the field of operations.

You mean to say you didn't know?

But nobody talked. A push was achieved or it wasn't. A miniature flag moved on the map. Men lost, and losses imposed on the government forces were recorded. There were some reverses. A huge airlift of supplies and matériel by the neighbouring African state allied in the cause of destabilization was successful; the rebel force would fight on for years, village by village, bridge by bridge, power stations and strategic roads gained on the map. There would be victory on the righteous side.

Nobody said how it was being done. The black government spread reports of massacres because it was losing, and of course the leftist and liberal press took up the tales. Intelligence, tuned to the clock with its gilded cupids, filed these: under disinformation about destabilization.

Here, always, they waited for him to go on. He swallowed continually between phrases, and while he was telling they would watch him swallow. The cold egg won't go down. There is a thin streamer of minute ants who come up six floors through the empty foyer and the closed reception rooms and find their way along the leg of the table to food left there; he knows. And telling, telling—telling over and over to himself, now that no one comes to ask any more, he swallows, while the ants come steadily. Go on, go on.

It wasn't until I went to the neighbouring State—it is a white state and very advanced—that provided the matériel, planes, intelligence supplied by its agents to the communications centre it set up for us in the house in Europe. There was also a base.

Go on.

A training base for our people. It was secret, no one knew it was there. Hidden in a game reserve. I was very confident—pleased—to find myself sent not only around Europe, but chosen to go to that State. To liaise. To meet the Commander of National Security and Special Services there. See for myself the important extent of co-operation in our mutual dedication to the cause. Report back on the morale of our men being trained there in the use of advanced weapons and strategy.

Yes?

A crescendo comes in great waves from the speaker provided with the tape player: to win the war, stabilize by destabilization, set up a regime of peace and justice!

During press conferences, at this point an ooze of heat would rise under his skin. Their eyes on him drew it up from his tissues like a blister. And then?

There's no one in the room, the curtains are closed against everyone. Swallow. I saw the male refugees captured at the border brought in starving. I saw how to deal with them. They were made to join our forces or were put back over the border to die. I could see that they would die. Their villages burned, their families hacked to death—you saw in their faces and bodies how it really happened . . . the disinformation. It wasn't talked about at that base, either. Our allies, at the dinners they gave—game dishes and wine, everything of the best provided, treated like a VIP—they didn't talk about these things. Well . . . I was shown around . . . everything. The secret radio station that broadcast the Voice of our organization. The latest weapons made available to us. The boots and uniforms made in their factories. (That outfit of mine must have come from there.) The planes taking off at night to fly our men, armed and equipped to do what they were trained to do. I knew, now, what that was.

Yes?

Of course, it was war...

So?

...War isn't pretty. There is brutality on both sides. I had to understand. Tried to. But planes also came back from over the border at night. Not empty. They carried what I thought were refugee children to be saved from the fighting; girls of twelve or thirteen, terrified, they had to be pulled apart from each other to get them to walk. They were brought in for the men who were receiving their military training. Men who had been without women; to satisfy them. After dinner, the Commander offered me one. He had one led in for himself. He took off her clothes to show me.

So, yes, I knew what happened to those girl children. I knew that our army had become—maybe always was—yes, what you say, a murderous horde that burned hospitals, cut off the ears of villagers, raped, blew up trains full of workers. Brought to devastation this country where I was born. It's there, only the glowing curtains keep it out. At night, when the curtains are drawn back it is still there in the dark with the blind bulk of buildings, the traces of broken boulevards and decayed squares marked in feeble lights. Familiar to me, can't say I don't know it, can't say it doesn't recognize me. It is there, with the sun pressing against the window, a population become beggars living in the streets, camping out in what used to be our—white people's—apartments, no electricity, no water in the tiled bathrooms, no glass in the windows, and on the fine balconies facing the sea where we used to take our aperitifs, those little open fires where they cook their scraps of food.

And that's the end.

But it's gone over again and again. No end. It's only the tape that ends. Can't be explained how someone begins really to know. Instead of having intelligence by fax and satellite.

Back in the room in Europe with its telecommunications there was on record the whereabouts of this black regime's representatives abroad. One day he went there. In the rebel army's outfit, with the beard, so that they could shoot him if they wanted; so that they would realize who he was and what he knew. Not the atrocities. Something else; all that he could offer to efface his knowledge of the atrocities: complete information about the rebel army, its leaders, its internal feuds, its allies, its sources of supply, the exact position and function of its secret bases. Everything. Everything he was and had been, right back to the jump with the parachute and the photograph of the tower. They didn't shoot. They kept him under guard so that the people from the telecommunications headquarters in the room with the antique clock would not kill him before he could tell. They handled him carefully; himself a strange and rare species, kept captured for study. They were aware of its worth, to them.

Debriefing is like destabilization, the term doesn't describe the method and experience. Day by day, divested of the boots, fatigues, the beret and the beard, first-class flights, the house in Europe, the dinners of honour, the prestige of intelligence—his life. He has been discovered there beneath it, sitting quite still on a chair in a dark room, only a naked full neck pulsating. In the silence after the tape ends it is possible to think there is the distinct sound of ants moving in an unwavering path.

They knew they couldn't have it for nothing—his life. They haven't provided the house with a garden that was part of the deal. Or the car. Of course, he can go out. Go where he likes, it was only for the first six months that he was restricted. Once they know they can trust him, he's not of interest to them any longer. Nothing more, now, to lead them to. Once he's told everything, once he's been displayed, what use is he to them?

They are right. Perhaps they will never come to him again.

The girl emerges from the bedroom, she sleeps late.

There is a girl. They didn't supply her. But they might have; she was there in the waiting room when he went under surveillance to a doctor. He politely let her take her turn with the doctor first, and when she came out they got talking. I don't see how I'm ever supposed to follow this diet, she said, what can you buy if you haven't got foreign currency—you know how it is, living here.

Yes—for the first time he saw it was so: he lives here. Perhaps it was possible for him to get what she needed? She didn't ask questions; access to foreign currency is not a subject to be discussed.

The girl's been in the bedroom all morning, just as if there was no one there. Now the dim room prolongs her lassitude, no break between night and day. Pink feet with hammer toes drag over the floor; she makes tasting sounds with her tongue against her palate. She takes a deep breath, holds then expels it; because he doesn't speak.

So you don't want to eat?

She has lifted the covering plate and touches the yellow mound of the yolk with her forefinger; the congealed surface dents shinily. She wipes her finger on the T-shirt that is her nightgown. A sprig of houseplant she brought and put in a glass, one day, is on the table where she set it down then; in the cloudy water, the darkened room, it has sent out one frail, floating thread of root. Ants are wavering at the rim of the glass. The thin buttermilk smell of her fluids and his semen comes to him as she bends to follow the ants' trail from the floor. After he had finished with her, last night, she said: You don't love me.

He was assailed by the sight of the twelve-year-old child and the Commander.

Then she heard something she couldn't believe. The man weeping. She drew away in fear and repugnance to the side of the bed.

She hangs about the room behind him, this morning, knowing he's not going to speak.

Why don't we go to the beach. Let's have a swim. I'd love to go and eat some prawns. We can take a bus. There's a good place ... it's cheap. And don't you feel like a swim, I'm dying to get into the water ... come on.

She waits patiently.

Has he shaken his head—there was some slight movement. There is nothing in the room she can turn to as a pretext to keep her there, waiting to see if he accepts her forgiveness, her humble understanding of her function. After a few minutes she goes back into the bedroom and comes out dressed.

I'm going. (Qualifies:) Going for a swim.

This time he nods and leans to take a cigarette.

She hasn't opened the door yet. She's hesitating, as if she thinks she ought to make some gesture, doesn't know what, might come over and touch his hair.

She's gone.

After the inhalation of the cigarette has become his breath and body, he gets up and goes to the window. He pulls aside the curtains to left and right. They are parched and faded, burned out. And now he is exposed: there is the bright stare of the beggared city, city turned inside out, no shelter there for life, the old men propped against empty façades to die, the orphaned children running in packs round the rubbish dumps, the men without ears and women with a stump where there was an arm, their clamour rising at him, rising six floors in the sun. He can't go out because they are all around him, the people.

Jump. The stunning blow of the earth as it came up to flexed knees, the parachute sinking silken.

He stands, and then backs into the room.

Not now; not yet.

Once Upon a Time

Someone has written to ask me to contribute to an anthology of stories for children. I reply that I don't write children's stories; and he writes back that at a recent congress/book fair/seminar a certain novelist said every writer ought to write at least one story for children. I think of sending a postcard saying I don't accept that I 'ought' to write anything.

And then last night I woke up—or rather was wakened without knowing what had roused me.

A voice in the echo-chamber of the subconscious?

A sound.

A creaking of the kind made by the weight carried by one foot after another along a wooden floor. I listened. I felt the apertures of my ears distend with concentration. Again: the creaking. I was waiting for it; waiting to hear if it indicated that feet were moving from room to room, coming up the passage—to my door. I have no burglar bars, no gun under the pillow, but I have the same fears as people who do take these precautions, and my windowpanes are thin as rime, could shatter like a wineglass. A woman was murdered (how do they put it) in broad daylight in a house two blocks away, last year, and the fierce dogs who guarded an old widower and his collection of antique clocks were strangled before he was knifed by a casual labourer he had dismissed without pay.

I was staring at the door, making it out in my mind rather than seeing it, in the dark. I lay quite still—a victim already—but the arrhythmia of my heart was fleeing, knocking this way and that against its body-cage. How finely tuned the senses are, just out of rest, sleep! I could never listen intently as that in the distractions of the day; I was reading every faintest sound, identifying and classifying its possible threat.

But I learned that I was to be neither threatened nor spared. There was no human weight pressing on the boards, the creaking was a buckling, an epicentre of stress. I was in it. The house that surrounds me while I sleep is built on undermined ground; far beneath my bed, the floor, the house's foundations, the stopes and passages of gold mines have hollowed the rock, and when some face trembles, detaches and falls, three thousand feet below, the whole house shifts slightly, bringing uneasy strain to the balance and counterbalance of brick, cement, wood and glass that hold it as a structure around me. The misbeats of my heart tailed off like the last muffled flourishes on one of the wooden xylophones made by the Chopi and Tsonga migrant miners who might have been down there, under me in the earth at that moment. The stope where the fall was could have been disused, dripping water from its ruptured veins; or men might now be interred there in the most profound of tombs.

I couldn't find a position in which my mind would let go of my body—release me to sleep again. So I began to tell myself a story; a bedtime story.

In a house, in a suburb, in a city, there were a man and his wife who loved each other very much and were living happily ever after. They had a little boy, and they loved him very much. They had a cat and a dog that the little boy loved very much. They had a car and a caravan trailer for holidays, and a swimming-pool which was fenced so that the little boy and his playmates would not fall in and drown. They had a housemaid who was absolutely trustworthy and an itinerant gardener who was highly recommended by the neighbours. For when they began to live happily ever after they were warned, by that wise old witch, the husband's mother, not to take on anyone off the street. They were inscribed in a medical benefit society, their pet dog was licensed, they were insured against fire, flood damage and theft, and subscribed to the local Neighbourhood Watch, which supplied them with a plaque for their gates lettered YOU HAVE BEEN WARNED over the silhouette of a would-be intruder. He was masked; it could not be said if he was black or white, and therefore proved the property owner was no racist.

It was not possible to insure the house, the swimming pool or the car against riot damage. There were riots, but these were outside the city, where people of another colour were quartered. These people were not allowed into the suburb except as reliable housemaids and gardeners, so there was nothing to fear, the husband told the wife. Yet she was afraid that some day such people might come up the street and tear off the plaque YOU HAVE BEEN

WARNED and open the gates and stream in . . . Nonsense, my dear, said the husband, there are police and soldiers and tear-gas and guns to keep them away. But to please her—for he loved her very much and buses were being burned, cars stoned, and schoolchildren shot by the police in those quarters out of sight and hearing of the suburb— he had electronically-controlled gates fitted. Anyone who pulled off the sign YOU HAVE BEEN WARNED and tried to open the gates would have to announce his intentions by pressing a button and speaking into a receiver relayed to the house. The little boy was fascinated by the device and used it as a walkie-talkie in cops and robbers play with his small friends.

The riots were suppressed, but there were many bur- glaries in the suburb and somebody's trusted housemaid was tied up and shut in a cupboard by thieves while she was in charge of her employers' house. The trusted house- maid of the man and wife and little boy was so upset by this misfortune befalling a friend left, as she herself often was, with responsibility for the possessions of the man and his wife and the little boy that she implored her employers to have burglar bars attached to the doors and windows of the house, and an alarm system installed. The wife said, She is right, let us take heed of her advice. So from every window and door in the house where they were living hap- pily ever after they now saw the trees and sky through bars, and when the little boy's pet cat tried to climb in by the fanlight to keep him company in his little bed at night, as it customarily had done, it set off the alarm keening through the house.

The alarm was often answered—it seemed—by other bur- glar alarms, in other houses, that had been triggered by pet cats or nibbling mice. The alarms called to one another across the gardens in shrills and bleats and wails that everyone soon became accustomed to, so that the din roused the inhabitants of the suburb no more than the croak of frogs and musical grating of cicadas' legs. Under cover of the electronic harpies' discourse intruders sawed the iron bars and broke into homes, taking away hi-fi equipment, television sets, cassette players, cameras and radios, jewellery and clothing, and sometimes were hungry enough to devour everything in the refrigerator or paused audaciously to drink the whisky in the cabinets or patio bars. Insurance companies paid no compensation for single malt, a loss made keener by the property owner's knowledge that the thieves wouldn't even have been able to appreciate what it was they were drinking.

Then the time came when many of the people who were not trusted housemaids and gardeners hung about the suburb because they were unemployed. Some importuned for a job: weeding or painting a roof; anything, *baas*, madam. But the man and his wife remembered the warning about taking on anyone off the street. Some drank liquor and fouled the street with discarded bottles. Some begged, waiting for the man or his wife to drive the car out of the electronically-operated gates. They sat about with their feet in the gutters, under the jacaranda trees that made a green tunnel of the street—for it was a beautiful suburb, spoilt only by their presence—and sometimes they fell asleep lying right before the gates in the midday sun. The wife could never see anyone go hungry. She sent the trusted housemaid out with bread and tea, but the trusted housemaid said these were loafers and *tsotsis*, who would come and tie her up and shut her in a cupboard. The husband said,

She's right. Take heed of her advice. You only encourage them with your bread and tea. They are looking for their chance...And he brought the little boy's tricycle from the garden into the house every night, because if the house was surely secure, once locked and with the alarm set, someone might still be able to climb over the wall or the electronically-closed gates into the garden.

You are right, said the wife, then the wall should be higher. And the wise old witch, the husband's mother, paid for the extra bricks as her Christmas present to her son and his wife—the little boy got a Space Man outfit and a book of fairy tales.

But every week there were more reports of intrusion: in broad daylight and the dead of night, in the early hours of the morning, and even in the lovely summer twilight—a certain family was at dinner while the bedrooms were being ransacked upstairs. The man and his wife, talking of the latest armed robbery in the suburb, were distracted by the sight of the little boy's pet cat effortlessly arriving over the seven-foot wall, descending first with a rapid bracing of extended forepaws down on the sheer vertical surface, and then a graceful launch, landing with swishing tail within the property. The whitewashed wall was marked with the cat's comings and goings; and on the street side of the wall there were larger red-earth smudges that could have been made by the kind of broken running shoes, seen on the feet of unemployed loiterers, that had no innocent destination.

When the man and wife and little boy took the pet dog for its walk round the neighbourhood streets they no longer paused to admire this show of roses or that perfect lawn; these were hidden behind an array of different varieties of security fences, walls and devices. The man, wife, little boy and dog passed a remarkable choice: there was the low-cost option of pieces of broken glass embedded in cement along the top of walls, there were iron grilles ending in lance-points, there were attempts at reconciling the aesthetics of prison architecture with the Spanish Villa style (spikes painted pink) and with the plaster urns of neo-classical façades (twelve-inch pikes finned like zigzags of lightning and painted pure white). Some walls had a small board affixed, giving the name and telephone number of the firm responsible for the installation of the devices. While the little boy and the pet dog raced ahead, the husband and wife found themselves comparing the possible effectiveness of each style against its appearance; and after several weeks when they paused before this barricade or that without needing to speak, both came out with the conclusion that only one was worth considering. It was the ugliest but the most honest in its suggestion of the pure concentration-camp style, no frills, all evident efficacy. Placed the length of walls, it consisted of a continuous coil of stiff and shining metal serrated into jagged blades, so that there would be no way of climbing over it and no way through its tunnel without getting entangled in its fangs. There would be no way out, only a struggle getting bloodier and bloodier, a deeper and sharper hooking and tearing of flesh. The wife shuddered to look at it. You're right, said the husband, anyone would think twice... And they took heed of the advice on a small board fixed to the wall: Consult DRAGON'S TEETH The People For Total Security.

Next day a gang of workmen came and stretched the razor-bladed coils all round the walls of the house where the husband and wife and little boy and pet dog and cat were living happily ever after. The sunlight flashed and slashed, off the serrations, the cornice of razor thorns encircled the home, shining. The husband said, Never mind. It will weather. The wife said, You're wrong. They guarantee it's rust-proof. And she waited until the little boy had run off to play before she said, I hope the cat will take heed... The husband said, Don't worry, my dear, cats always look before they leap. And it was true that from that day on the cat slept in the little boy's bed and kept to the garden, never risking a try at breaching security.

One evening, the mother read the little boy to sleep with a fairy story from the book the wise old witch had given him at Christmas. Next day he pretended to be the Prince who braves the terrible thicket of thorns to enter the palace and kiss the Sleeping Beauty back to life: he dragged a ladder to the wall, the shining coiled tunnel was just wide enough for his little body to creep in, and with the first fixing of its razor-teeth in his knees and hands and head he screamed and struggled deeper into its tangle. The trusted housemaid and the itinerant gardener, whose 'day' it was, came running, the first to see and to scream with him, and the itinerant gardener tore his hands trying to get at the little boy. Then the man and his wife burst wildly into the garden and for some reason (the cat, probably) the alarm set up wailing against the screams while the bleeding mass of the little boy was hacked out of the security coil with saws, wire-cutters, choppers, and they carried it—the man, the wife, the hysterical trusted housemaid and the weeping gardener—into the house.

The Ultimate Safari

*The African Adventure Lives On... You can do it!
The ultimate safari or expedition
with leaders who <u>know</u> Africa.*

—TRAVEL ADVERTISEMENT,

Observer, LONDON, 27/11/88

That night our mother went to the shop and she didn't come back. Ever. What happened? I don't know. My father also had gone away one day and never come back; but he was fighting in the war. We were in the war, too, but we were children, we were like our grandmother and grandfather, we didn't have guns. The people my father was fighting—the bandits, they are called by our government—ran all over the place and we ran away from them like chickens chased by dogs. We didn't know where to go. Our mother went to the shop because someone said you could get some oil for cooking. We were happy because we hadn't tasted oil for a long time; perhaps she got the oil and someone knocked her down in the dark and took that oil from her. Perhaps she met the bandits. If you meet them, they will kill you. Twice they came to our village and we ran and hid in the bush and when they'd gone we came back and found they had taken everything; but the third time they came back there was nothing to take, no oil, no food, so they burned the thatch and the roofs of our houses fell in. My mother found some pieces of tin and we put those up over part of the house. We were waiting there for her that night she never came back.

We were frightened to go out, even to do our business, because the bandits did come. Not into our house—without a roof it must have looked as if there was no one in it, everything gone—but all through the village. We heard people screaming and running. We were afraid even to run, without our mother to tell us where. I am the middle one, the girl, and my little brother clung against my stomach with his arms round my neck and his legs round my waist like a baby monkey to its mother. All night my first-born brother kept in his hand a broken piece of wood from one of our burnt house-poles. It was to save himself if the bandits found him.

We stayed there all day. Waiting for her. I don't know what day it was; there was no school, no church any more in our village, so you didn't know whether it was a Sunday or a Monday.

When the sun was going down, our grandmother and grandfather came. Someone from our village had told them we children were alone, our mother had not come back. I say 'grandmother' before 'grandfather' because it's like that: our grandmother is big and strong, not yet old, and our grandfather is small, you don't know where he is, in his loose trousers, he smiles but he hasn't heard what you're saying, and his hair looks as if he's left it full of soap suds. Our grandmother took us—me, the baby, my first-born brother, our grandfather—back to her house and we were all afraid (except the baby, asleep on our grandmother's back) of meeting the bandits on the way. We waited a long time at our grandmother's place. Perhaps it was a month. We were hungry. Our mother never came. While we were waiting for her to fetch us our grandmother had no food for us, no food for our grandfather and herself. A woman with milk in her breasts gave us some for my little brother, although at our house he used to eat porridge, same as we did. Our grandmother took us to look for wild spinach but everyone else in her village did the same and there wasn't a leaf left.

Our grandfather, walking a little behind some young men, went to look for our mother but didn't find her. Our grandmother cried with other women and I sang the hymns with them. They brought a little food—some beans—but after two days there was nothing again. Our grandfather used to have three sheep and a cow and a vegetable garden but the bandits had long ago taken the sheep and the cow, because they were hungry, too; and when planting time came our grandfather had no seed to plant.

So they decided—our grandmother did; our grandfather made little noises and rocked from side to side, but she took no notice—we would go away. We children were pleased. We wanted to go away from where our mother wasn't and where we were hungry. We wanted to go where there were no bandits and there was food. We were glad to think there must be such a place; away.

Our grandmother gave her church clothes to someone in exchange for some dried mealies and she boiled them and tied them in a rag. We took them with us when we went and she thought we would get water from the rivers but we didn't come to any river and we got so thirsty we had to turn back. Not all the way to our grandparents' place but to a village where there was a pump. She opened the basket where she carried some clothes and the mealies and she sold her shoes to buy a big plastic container for water. I said, *Gogo*, how will you go to church now even without shoes, but she said we had a long journey and too much to carry. At that village we met other people who were also going away. We joined them because they seemed to know where that was better than we did.

To get there we had to go through the Kruger Park. We knew about the Kruger Park. A kind of whole country of animals—elephants, lions, jackals, hyenas, hippos, crocodiles, all kinds of animals. We had some of them in our own country, before the war (our grandfather remembers; we children weren't born yet) but the bandits kill the elephants and sell their tusks, and the bandits and our soldiers have eaten all the buck. There was a man in our village without legs—a crocodile took them off, in our river; but all the same our country is a country of people, not animals. We knew about the Kruger Park because some of our men used to leave home to work there in the places where white people come to stay and look at the animals.

So we started to go away again. There were women and other children like me who had to carry the small ones on their backs when the women got tired. A man led us into the Kruger Park; are we there yet, are we there yet, I kept asking our grandmother. Not yet, the man said, when she asked him for me. He told us we had to take a long way to get round the fence, which he explained would kill you, roast off your skin the moment you touched it, like the wires high up on poles that give electric light in our towns. I've seen that sign of a head without eyes or skin or hair on an iron box at the mission hospital we used to have before it was blown up.

When I asked the next time, they said we'd been walking in the Kruger Park for an hour. But it looked just like the bush we'd been walking through all day, and we hadn't seen any animals except the monkeys and birds which live around us at home, and a tortoise that, of course, couldn't get away from us. My first-born brother and the other boys brought it to the man so it could be killed and we could cook and eat it. He let it go because he told us we could not make a fire; all the time we were in the Park we must not make a fire because the smoke would show we were there. Police, wardens, would come and send us back where we came from. He said we must move like animals among the animals, away from the roads, away from the white people's camps. And at that moment I heard—I'm sure I was the first to hear—cracking branches and the sound of something parting grasses and I almost squealed because I thought it was the police, wardens—the people he was telling us to look out for—who had found us already. And it was an elephant, and another elephant, and more elephants, big blots of dark moved wherever you looked between the trees. They were curling their trunks round the red leaves of the Mopane trees and stuffing them into their mouths. The babies leant against their mothers. The almost grown-up ones wrestled like my first-born brother with his friends—only they used trunks instead of arms. I was so interested I forgot to be afraid. The man said we should just stand still and be quiet while the elephants passed. They passed very slowly because elephants are too big to need to run from anyone.

The buck ran from us. They jumped so high they seemed to fly. The warthogs stopped dead, when they heard us, and swerved off the way a boy in our village used to zigzag on the bicycle his father had brought back from the mines. We followed the animals to where they drank. When they had gone, we went to their water-holes. We were never thirsty without finding water, but the animals ate, ate all the time. Whenever you saw them they were eating, grass, trees, roots. And there was nothing for us. The mealies were finished. The only food we could eat was what the baboons ate, dry little figs full of ants that grow along the branches of the trees at the rivers. It was hard to be like the animals.

When it was very hot during the day we would find lions lying asleep. They were the colour of the grass and we didn't see them at first but the man did, and he led us back and a long way round where they slept. I wanted to lie down like the lions. My little brother was getting thin but he was very heavy. When our grandmother looked for me, to put him on my back, I tried not to see. My first-born brother stopped talking; and when we rested he had to be shaken to get up again, as if he was just like our grandfather, he couldn't hear. I saw flies crawling on our grandmother's face and she didn't brush them off; I was frightened. I picked a palm leaf and chased them.

We walked at night as well as by day. We could see the fires where the white people were cooking in the camps and we could smell the smoke and the meat. We watched the hyenas with their backs that slope as if they're ashamed, slipping through the bush after the smell. If one turned its head, you saw it had big brown shining eyes like our own, when we looked at each other in the dark. The wind brought voices in our own language from the compounds where the people who work in the camps live. A woman among us wanted to go to them at night and ask them to help us. They can give us the food from the dustbins, she said, she started wailing and our grandmother had to grab her and put a hand over her mouth. The man who led us had told us that we must keep out of the way of our people who worked at the Kruger Park; if they helped us they would lose their work. If they saw us, all they could do was pretend we were not there; they had seen only animals.

Sometimes we stopped to sleep for a little while at night. We slept close together. I don't know which night it was—because we were walking, walking, any time, all the time—we heard the lions very near. Not groaning loudly the way they did far off. Panting, like we do when we run, but it's a different kind of panting: you can hear they're not running, they're waiting, somewhere near. We all rolled closer together, on top of each other, the ones on the edge fighting to get into the middle. I was squashed against a woman who smelled bad because she was afraid but I was glad to hold tight on to her. I prayed to God to make the lions take someone on the edge and go. I shut my eyes not to see the tree from which a lion might jump right into the middle of us, where I was. The man who led us jumped up instead, and beat on the tree with a dead branch. He had taught us never to make a sound but he shouted. He shouted at the lions like a drunk man shouting at nobody, in our village. The lions went away. We heard them groaning, shouting back at him from far off.

We were tired, so tired. My first-born brother and the man had to lift our grandfather from stone to stone where we found places to cross the rivers. Our grandmother is strong but her feet were bleeding. We could not carry the basket on our heads any longer, we couldn't carry anything except my little brother. We left our things under a bush. As long as our bodies get there, our grandmother said. Then we ate some wild fruit we didn't know from home and our stomachs ran. We were in the grass called elephant grass because it is nearly as tall as an elephant, that day we had those pains, and our grandfather couldn't just get down in front of people like my little brother, he went off into the grass to be on his own. We had to keep up, the man who led us always kept telling us, we must catch up, but we asked him to wait for our grandfather.

So everyone waited for our grandfather to catch up. But he didn't. It was the middle of the day; insects were singing in our ears and we couldn't hear him moving through the grass. We couldn't see him because the grass was so high and he was so small. But he must have been somewhere there inside his loose trousers and his shirt that was torn and our grandmother couldn't sew because she had no cotton. We knew he couldn't have gone far because he was weak and slow. We all went to look for him, but in groups, so we too wouldn't be hidden from each other in that grass. It got into our eyes and noses; we called him softly but the noise of the insects must have filled the little space left for hearing in his ears. We looked and looked but we couldn't find him. We stayed in that long grass all night. In my sleep I found him curled round in a place he had tramped down for himself, like the places we'd seen where the buck hide their babies.

When I woke up he still wasn't anywhere. So we looked again, and by now there were paths we'd made by going through the grass many times, it would be easy for him to find us if we couldn't find him. All that day we just sat and waited. Everything is very quiet when the sun is on your head, inside your head, even if you lie, like the animals, under the trees. I lay on my back and saw those ugly birds with hooked beaks and plucked necks flying round and round above us. We had passed them often where they were feeding on the bones of dead animals, nothing was ever left there for us to eat. Round and round, high up and then lower down and then high again. I saw their necks poking to this side and that. Flying round and round. I saw our grandmother, who sat up all the time with my little brother on her lap, was seeing them, too.

In the afternoon the man who led us came to our grandmother and told her the other people must move on. He said, If their children don't eat soon they will die.

Our grandmother said nothing.

I'll bring you water before we go, he told her.

Our grandmother looked at us, me, my first-born brother, and my little brother on her lap. We watched the other people getting up to leave. I didn't believe the grass would be empty, all around us, where they had been. That we would be alone in this place, the Kruger Park, the police or the animals would find us. Tears came out of my eyes and nose onto my hands but our grandmother took no notice. She got up, with her feet apart the way she puts them when she is going to lift firewood, at home in our village, she swung my little brother onto her back, tied him in her cloth—the top of her dress was torn and her big breasts were showing but there was nothing in them for him. She said, Come.

So we left the place with the long grass. Left behind. We went with the others and the man who led us. We started to go away, again.

There's a very big tent, bigger than a church or a school, tied down to the ground. I didn't understand that was what it would be, when we got there, away. I saw a thing like that the time our mother took us to the town because she heard our soldiers were there and she wanted to ask them if they knew where our father was. In that tent, people were praying and singing. This one is blue and white like that one but it's not for praying and singing, we live in it with other people who've come from our country. Sister from the clinic says we're two hundred without counting the babies, and we have new babies, some were born on the way through the Kruger Park.

Inside, even when the sun is bright it's dark and there's a kind of whole village in there. Instead of houses each family has a little place closed off with sacks or cardboard from boxes—whatever we can find—to show the other families it's yours and they shouldn't come in even though there's no door and no windows and no thatch, so that if you're standing up and you're not a small child you can see into everybody's house. Some people have even made paint from ground rocks and drawn designs on the sacks.

Of course, there really is a roof—the tent is the roof, far, high up. It's like a sky. It's like a mountain and we're inside it; through the cracks paths of dust lead down, so thick you think you could climb them. The tent keeps off the rain overhead but the water comes in at the sides and in the little streets between our places—you can only move along them one person at a time—the small kids like my little brother play in the mud. You have to step over them. My little brother doesn't play. Our grandmother takes him to the clinic when the doctor comes on Mondays. Sister says there's something wrong with his head, she thinks it's because we didn't have enough food at home. Because of the war. Because our father wasn't there. And then because he was so hungry in the Kruger Park. He likes just to lie about

on our grandmother all day, on her lap or against her somewhere, and he looks at us and looks at us. He wants to ask
something but you can see he can't. If I tickle him he may
just smile. The clinic gives us special powder to make into
porridge for him and perhaps one day he'll be all right.

When we arrived we were like him—my first-born
brother and I. I can hardly remember. The people who live
in the village near the tent took us to the clinic, it's where
you have to sign that you've come—away, through the
Kruger Park. We sat on the grass and everything was mud-
dled. One Sister was pretty with her hair straightened and
beautiful high-heeled shoes and she brought us the special
powder. She said we must mix it with water and drink it
slowly. We tore the packets open with our teeth and licked
it all up, it stuck round my mouth and I sucked it from my
lips and fingers. Some other children who had walked with
us vomited. But I only felt everything in my belly moving,
the stuff going down and around like a snake, and hiccups
hurt me. Another Sister called us to stand in line on the
verandah of the clinic but we couldn't. We sat all over the
place there, falling against each other; the Sisters helped
each of us up by the arm and then stuck a needle in it.
Other needles drew our blood into tiny bottles. This was
against sickness, but I didn't understand, every time my
eyes dropped closed I thought I was walking, the grass was
long, I saw the elephants, I didn't know we were away.

But our grandmother was still strong, she could still stand
up, she knows how to write and she signed for us. Our
grandmother got us this place in the tent against one of the
sides, it's the best kind of place there because although the
rain comes in, we can lift the flap when the weather is good
and then the sun shines on us, the smells in the tent go

out. Our grandmother knows a woman here who showed her where there is good grass for sleeping mats, and our grandmother made some for us. Once every month the food truck comes to the clinic. Our grandmother takes along one of the cards she signed and when it has been punched we get a sack of mealie meal. There are wheelbarrows to take it back to the tent; my first-born brother does this for her and then he and the other boys have races, steering the empty wheelbarrows back to the clinic. Sometimes he's lucky and a man who's bought beer in the village gives him money to deliver it—though that's not allowed, you're supposed to take that wheelbarrow straight back to the Sisters. He buys a cold drink and shares it with me if I catch him. On another day, every month, the church leaves a pile of old clothes in the clinic yard. Our grandmother has another card to get punched, and then we can choose something: I have two dresses, two pants and a jersey, so I can go to school.

The people in the village have let us join their school. I was surprised to find they speak our language; our grandmother told me, That's why they allow us to stay on their land. Long ago, in the time of our fathers, there was no fence that kills you, there was no Kruger Park between them and us, we were the same people under our own king, right from our village we left to this place we've come to.

Now that we've been in the tent so long—I have turned eleven and my little brother is nearly three although he is so small, only his head is big, he's not come right in it yet—some people have dug up the bare ground around the tent and planted beans and mealies and cabbage. The old men weave branches to put up fences round their gardens. No one is allowed to look for work in the towns but some of the women have found work in the village and can buy things. Our grandmother, because she's still strong, finds work where people are building houses—in this village the people build nice houses with bricks and cement, not mud like we used to have at our home. Our grandmother carries bricks for these people and fetches baskets of stones on her head. And so she has money to buy sugar and tea and milk and soap. The store gave her a calendar she has hung up on our flap of the tent. I am clever at school and she collected advertising paper people throw away outside the store and covered my schoolbooks with it. She makes my first-born brother and me do our homework every afternoon before it gets dark because there is no room except to lie down, close together, just as we did in the Kruger Park, in our place in the tent, and candles are expensive. Our grandmother hasn't been able to buy herself a pair of shoes for church yet, but she has bought black school shoes and polish to clean them with for my first-born brother and me. Every morning, when people are getting up in the tent, the babies are crying, people are pushing each other at the taps outside and some children are already pulling the crusts of porridge off the pots we ate from last night, my first-born brother and I clean our shoes. Our grandmother makes us sit on our mats with our legs straight out so she can look carefully at our shoes to make sure we have done it properly. No other children in the tent have real school shoes. When we three look at them it's as if we are in a real house again, with no war, no away.

Some white people came to take photographs of our people living in the tent—they said they were making a film, I've never seen what that is though I know about it. A white woman squeezed into our space and asked our grandmother questions which were told to us in our language by someone who understands the white woman's.

How long have you been living like this?

She means here? our grandmother said. In this tent, two years and one month.

And what do you hope for the future?

Nothing. I'm here.

But for your children?

I want them to learn so that they can get good jobs and money.

Do you hope to go back to Mozambique—to your own country?

I will not go back.

But when the war is over—you won't be allowed to stay here? Don't you want to go home?

I didn't think our grandmother wanted to speak again. I didn't think she was going to answer the white woman. The white woman put her head on one side and smiled at us.

Our grandmother looked away from her and spoke— There is nothing. No home.

Why does our grandmother say that? Why? I'll go back. I'll go back through that Kruger Park. After the war, if there are no bandits any more, our mother may be waiting for us. And maybe when we left our grandfather, he was only left behind, he found his way somehow, slowly, through the Kruger Park, and he'll be there. They'll be home, and I'll remember them.

A Find

To hell with them.

A man who had bad luck with women decided to live alone for a while. He was twice married for love. He cleared the house of whatever his devoted second wife had somehow missed out when she left with the favourite possessions they had collected together—paintings, rare glass, even the best wines lifted from the cellar. He threw away books on whose flyleaf the first wife had lovingly written her new name as a bride. Then he went on holiday without taking some woman along. For the first time he could remember; but those tarts and tramps with whom he had believed himself to be in love had turned out unfaithful as the honest wives who had vowed to cherish him forever.

He went alone to a resort where the rocks flung up the sea in ragged fans, the tide sizzled and sucked in the pools. There was no sand. On stones like boiled sweets, striped and flecked and veined, people—women—lay on salt-faded mattresses and caressed themselves with scented oils. Their hair was piled up and caught in elastic garlands of artificial flowers, that year, or dripped—as they came out of the water with crystal beads studding glossy limbs—from gilt clasps that flashed back and forth to the hoops looped in their ears. Their breasts were bared. They wore inverted triangles of luminescent cloth over the pubis, secured by a string that went up through the divide of the buttocks to meet two strings coming round from over the belly and hip-bones. In his line of vision, as they walked away down to the sea they appeared totally naked; when they came up out of the sea, gasping with pleasure, coming towards his line of vision, their breasts danced, drooped as the women bent, laughing, for towels and combs and the anointing oil. The bodies of some were patterned like tie-dyed fabric: strips and patches white or red where garments had covered bits of them from the fiery immersion of sun. The nipples of others were raw as strawberries, it could be observed that they could scarcely bear to touch them with balm. There were men, but he didn't see men. When he closed his eyes and listened to the sea he could smell the women—the oil.

He swam a great deal. Far out in the calm bay between wind-surfers crucified against their gaudy sails, closer in shore where the surf trampled his head under hordes of white waters. A shoal of young mothers carried their infants about in the shallows. Denting its softness, naked against their mothers' flesh the children clung, so lately separated from it that they still seemed part of those female bodies in which they had been planted by males like himself. He lay on the stones to dry. He liked the hard nudging of the stones, fidgeting till he adjusted his bones to them, wriggling them into depressions until his contours were contained rather than resisted. He slept. He woke to see their shaven legs passing his head—women. Drops shaken from their wet hair fell on his warm shoulders. Sometimes he found himself swimming underwater beneath them, his tough-skinned body grazing past like a shark.

As men do at the shore when they are alone, he flung stones at the sea, remembering—regaining—the art of making them skim and skip across the water. Lying face-down out of reach of the last rills, he sifted handfuls of sea-polished stones and, close up, began to see them as adults cease to see: the way a child will look and look at a flower, a leaf—a stone, following its alluvial stripes, its fragments of mysterious colour, its buried sprinklings of mica, feeling (he did) its egg- or lozenge-shape smoothed by the sea's oiled caressing hand.

Not all the stones were really stones. There were flattish amber ovals the gem-cutter ocean had buffed out of broken beer bottles. There were cabochons of blue and green glass (some other drowned bottle) that could have passed for aquamarines and emeralds. Children collected them in hats or buckets. And one afternoon among these treasures mixed with bits of Styrofoam discarded from cargo ships and other plastic jetsam that is cast, refloated and cast again, on shores all round the world, he found in the stones with which he was occupying his hand like a monk telling his beads, a real treasure. Among the pebbles of coloured glass was a diamond and sapphire ring. It was not on the surface of the stony beach, so evidently had not been dropped there that day by one of the women. Some darling, some rich man's treasure (or ensconced wife), diving off a yacht, out there, wearing her jewels while she fashionably jettisoned other coverings, must have felt one of the rings slipped from her finger by the water. Or didn't feel it, noticed the loss only when back on deck, rushed to find the insurance policy, while the sea drew the ring deeper and deeper down; and then, tiring of it over days, years, slowly pushed and washed it up to dump on land. It was a beautiful ring. The sapphire a large oblong surrounded by round diamonds with a baguette-cut diamond, set horizontally on either side of this brilliant mound, bridging it to an engraved circle.

Although it had been dug up from a good six inches down by his random fingering, he looked around as if the owner were sure to be standing over him.

But they were oiling themselves, they were towelling their infants, they were plucking their eyebrows in the reflection of tiny mirrors, they were sitting cross-legged with their breasts lolling above the squat tables where the waiter from the restaurant had placed their salads and bottles of white wine. He took the ring up to the restaurant; perhaps some-one had reported a loss. The patronne drew back. She might have been being offered stolen goods by a fence. It's valuable. Take it to the police.

Suspicion arouses alertness; perhaps, in this foreign place, there was some cause to be suspicious. Even of the police. If no one claimed the ring, some local would pocket it. So what was the difference—he put it into his own pocket, or rather into the shoulder-bag that held his money, his credit cards, his car keys and sunglasses. And he went back to the beach and lay down again, on the stones, among the women. To think.

He put an advertisement in the local paper. *Ring found on Blue Horizon Beach, Tuesday 1st,* and the telephone and room number at his hotel. The patronne was right; there were many calls. A few from men, claiming their wives, mothers, girl-friends had, indeed, lost a ring on that beach. When he asked them to describe the ring, they took a chance: a diamond ring. But they could only prevaricate when pressed for more details. If a woman's voice was the wheedling, ingratiating one (even weepy, some of them) recognizable as that of some middle-aged con-woman, he cut off the call the moment she tried to describe her lost ring. But if the voice was attractive and sometimes clearly young, soft, even hesitant in its lying boldness, he asked the owner to come to his hotel to identify the ring.

Describe it.

He seated them comfortably before his open balcony with the light from the sea interrogating their faces. Only one convinced him she really had lost a ring; she described it in detail and went away, sorry to have troubled him. Others—some quite charming or even extremely pretty, dressed to seduce—would have settled for something else come of the visit, if they could not get away with their invented descriptions of a ring. They seemed to calculate that a ring is a ring; if it's valuable, it must have diamonds, and one or two were ingenious enough to say, yes, there were other precious stones with it, but it was an heirloom (grandmother, aunt) and they didn't really know the names of the stones.

But the colour? The shape?

They left as if affronted; or they giggled guiltily, they'd come just for a dare, a bit of fun. And they were quite difficult to get rid of politely.

Then there was one with a voice unlike that of any of the other callers, the controlled voice of a singer or an actress, maybe, expressing diffidence. I have given up hope. Of finding it ... my ring. She had seen the advertisement and thought, no, no, it's no use. But if there were a million-to-one chance ... He asked her to come to the hotel.

She was certainly forty, a born beauty with great, still,

grey-green eyes and no help needed except to keep her hair peacock-black. It grew from a peak like a beak high on her round forehead and was drawn up to a coil on her crown, glossy as smoothed feathers. There was no sign of a fold where her breasts met, firmly spaced in the neck of a dress black as her hair. Her hands were made for rings; she spread long thumbs and fingers, turned palms out: And then it was gone, I saw a gleam a moment in the water—

Describe it.

She gazed straight at him, turned her head to direct those eyes away, and began to speak. Very elaborate, she said, platinum and gold . . . you know, it's difficult to be precise about an object you've worn so long you don't notice it any more. A large diamond . . . several. And emeralds, and red stones . . . rubies, but I think they had fallen out before . . .

He went to the drawer in the hotel desk-cum-dressing-table and from under folders describing restaurants, cable TV programmes and room service available, he took an envelope. Here's your ring, he said.

Her eyes did not change. He held it out to her.

Her hand wafted slowly towards him as if under water. She took the ring from him and began to put it on the middle finger of her right hand. It would not fit but she corrected the movement with swift conjuring and it slid home over the third finger.

He took her out to dinner and the subject was not referred to. Ever again. She became his third wife. They live together with no more unsaid, between them, than any other couple.

My Father Leaves Home

The houses turn aside, lengthwise from the village street, to be private. But they're painted with flowery and fruity scrolls and garlands. Blossoming vines are strung like washing along the narrow porches' diminishing perspective. Tomatoes and daisies climb together behind picket fences. Crowded in a slot of garden are pens and cages for chickens and ducks, and there's a pig. But not in the house he came from; there wouldn't have been a pig.

The post office is made of slatted wood with a carved valance under the roof—a post-office sign is recognizable anywhere, in any language, although it's one from a time before airmail: not a stylized bird but a curved post-horn with cord and tassels. It's from here that the letters would have gone, arranging the passage. There's a bench outside and an old woman sits there shelling peas. She's wearing a black scarf tied over her head and an apron, she has the lipless closed mouth of someone who has lost teeth. How old? The age of a woman without oestrogen pills, hair tint charts, sun-screen and anti-wrinkle creams. She packed for him. The clothes of a cold country, he had no other. She sewed up rents and darned socks; and what else? A cap, a coat; a boy of thirteen might not have owned a hand-me-down suit, yet. Or one might have been obtained specially for him, for the voyage, for the future.

Horse-drawn carts clomp and rattle along the streets. Wagons sway to the gait of fringe-hooved teams on the roads between towns, delaying cars and buses back into another century. He was hoisted to one of these carts with his bag, wearing the suit; certainly the cap. Boots newly mended by the member of the family whose trade this was. There must have been a shoemaker among them; that was the other choice open to him: he could have learnt shoe-making but had decided for watch-making. They must have equipped him with the loupe for his eye and the miniature screwdrivers and screws, the hairsprings, the fish-scale watch glasses; these would be in his bag as well. And some religious necessities. The shawl, the things to wind round his arm and brow. She wouldn't have forgotten those; he was thirteen, they had kept him home and fed him, at least until their religion said he was a man.

At the station the gypsies are singing in the bar. It's night. The train sweats a fog of steam in the autumn cold and he could be standing there somewhere, beside his bag, waiting to board. She might have come with him as far as this, but more likely not. When he clambered up to the cart, that was the end, for her. She never saw him again. The man with the beard, the family head, was there. He was the one who had saved for the train ticket and ship's passage. There are no farewells; there's no room for sorrow in the drunken joy of the gypsies filling the bar, the shack glows with their heat, a hearth in the dark of the night. The bearded man is going with his son to the sea, where the old life ends. He will find him a place in the lower levels of the ship, he will hand over the tickets and bits of paper that will tell the future who the boy was.

We had bought smoked paprika sausage and slivovitz for the trip—the party was too big to fit into one car, so it was more fun to take a train. Among the padded shotgun sleeves and embossed leather gun cases we sang and passed the bottle round, finding one another's remarks uproarious. The Frenchman had a nest of thimble-sized silver cups and he sliced the sausage towards his thumb, using a horn-handled knife from the hotel gift shop in the capital. The Englishman tried to read a copy of Cobbett's *Rural Rides* but it lay on his lap while the white liquor opened up in him unhappiness in his marriage, confided to a woman he had not met before. Restless with pleasure, people went in and out of the compartment, letting in a turned-up volume of motion and buffets of fresh air; outside, seen with a forehead resting against the corridor window, nothing but trees, trees, the twist of a river with a rotting boat, the fading Eastern European summer, distant from the sun.

Back inside to catch up with the party: someone was being applauded for producing a bottle of wine, someone else was taking teasing instruction on how to photograph with a newfangled camera. At the stations of towns nobody looked at—the same industrial intestines of factory yards and junk tips passed through by railway lines anywhere in the world we came from—local people boarded and sat on suitcases in the corridors. One man peered in persistently and the mood was to make room for him somehow in the compartment. Nobody could speak the language and he

couldn't speak ours, but the wine and sausage brought instant surprised communication, we talked to him whether
he could follow the words or not, and he shrugged and
smiled with the delighted and anguished responses of one
struck dumb by strangers. He asserted his position only by
waving away the slivovitz—that was what foreigners natu-
rally would feel obliged to drink. And when we forgot about
him while arguing over a curious map the State hunting
organization had given us, not ethno- or geographic but
showing the distribution of water- and wildfowl in the area
we were approaching, I caught him looking over us, one by
one, trying to read the lives we came from, uncertain, from
unfamiliar signs, whether to envy, to regard with cynicism,
or to be amused. He fell asleep. And I studied him.

There was no one from the hunting lodge come to meet
us at the village station ringed on the map. It was night.
Autumn cold. We stood about and stamped our feet in the
adventure of it. There was no station-master. A telephone
booth, but whom could we call upon? All inclusive; you will
be escorted by a guide and interpreter everywhere—so we
had not thought to take the telephone number of the lodge.
There was a wooden shack in the darkness, blurry with
thick yellow light and noise. A bar! The men of the party
went over to join the one male club that has reciprocal
membership everywhere; the women were uncertain
whether they would be acceptable—the customs of each
country have to be observed, in some you can bare your
breasts, in others you are indecent if wearing trousers. The
Englishman came back and forth to report. Men were having a wild time in the shack, they must be celebrating something, they were some kind of brotherhood, black-haired
and unshaven, drunk. We sat on our baggage in the mist
of steam left by the train, a dim caul of visibility lit by the

glow of the bar, and our world fell away sheer from the edge of the platform. Nothing. At an unknown stage of a journey to an unknown place, suddenly unimaginable.

An old car splashed into the station yard. The lodge manager fell out on his feet like a racing driver. He wore a green felt hat with badges and feathers fastened round the band. He spoke our language, yes. It's not good there, he said when the men of the party came out of the bar. You watch your pocket. Gypsies. They don't work, only steal, and make children so the government gives them money every time.

The moon on its back.

One of the first things he will have noticed when he arrived was that the moon in the Southern Hemisphere lies the wrong way round. The sun still rises in the east and sets in the west but the one other certainty to be counted on, that the same sky that covers the village covers the whole earth, is gone. What greater confirmation of how far away; as you look up, on the first night.

He might have learnt a few words on the ship. Perhaps someone who had preceded him by a year or so met him. He was put on a train that travelled for two days through vineyards and mountains and then the desert; but long before the ship landed already he must have been too hot in the suit, coming south. On the high plateau he arrived at the gold mines to be entrusted to a relative. The relative had been too proud to have explained by post that he was too poor to take him in but the wife made this clear. He took the watch-making tools he had been provided with and went to the mines. And then? He waylaid white miners and replaced balance wheels and broken watch-faces while-you-wait, he went to the compounds where black miners had proudly acquired watches as the manacles of their new slavery: to shift work. In this, their own country, they were migrants from their homes, like him. They had only a few words of the language, like him. While he picked up English he also picked up the terse jargon of English and their languages the miners were taught so that work orders could be understood. *Fanagalo*: 'Do this, do it like this'. A vocabulary of command. So straight away he knew that if he was poor and alien at least he was white, he spoke his broken phrases from the rank of the commanders to the commanded: the first indication of who he was, now. And the black miners' watches were mostly cheap ones not worth mending. They could buy a new one for the price he would have to ask for repairs; he bought a small supply of Zobo pocket watches and hawked them at the compounds. So it was because of the blacks he became a business man; another indication.

And then?

Zobos were fat metal circles with a stout ring at the top and a loud tick tramping out time. He had a corrugated-tin-roofed shop with his watch-maker's bench in a corner and watches, clocks and engagement and wedding rings for sale. The white miners were the ones whose custom it was to mark betrothals with adornments bought on the instalment plan. They promised to pay so-much-a-month; on the last Friday, when they had their wages, they came in from the hotel bar smelling of brandy. He taught himself to keep books and carried bad debts into the Depression of the Thirties.

He was married, with children, by then. Perhaps they had offered to send a girl out for him, a home girl with whom he could make love in his own language, who would cook according to the dietary rules. It was the custom for those from the villages; he surely could have afforded the fare. But if they knew he had left the tin shack behind the shop where he had slept when first he became a business man, surely they couldn't imagine him living in the local hotel where the white miners drank and he ate meat cooked by blacks. He took singing lessons and was inducted at the Masonic Lodge. Above the roll-top desk in the office behind his new shop, with its sign WATCHMAKER JEW- ELLER & SILVERSMITH, was an oval gilt-framed studio photograph of him in the apron of his Masonic rank. He made another move; he successfully courted a young woman whose mother tongue was English. From the village above which the moon turned the other way there came as a wedding gift only a strip of grey linen covered with silk embroidery in flowers and scrolls. The old woman who sat on the bench must have done the needlework long before, kept it for the anticipated occasion, because by the time of the distant marriage she was blind (so someone wrote). Injured in a pogrom—was that a supposition, an exagger- ation of woes back there, that those who had left all behind used to dramatize an escape? More likely cataracts, in that village, and no surgeon available. The granddaughters discovered the piece of embroidery stuck away behind lavender-scented towels and pillowcases in their mother's linen cupboard and used it as a carpet for their dolls' house.

The English wife played the piano and the children sang round her but he didn't sing. Apparently the lessons were given up; sometimes she laughed with friends over how he had been told he was a light baritone and at Masonic con- certs sang ballads with words by Tennyson. As if he knew who Tennyson was! By the time the younger daughter became curious about the photograph looking down behind its bulge of convex glass in the office, he had stopped going to Masonic meetings. Once he had driven into the garage wall when coming home from such an occasion; the damage was referred to in moments of tension, again and again. But perhaps he gave up that rank because when he got into bed beside his wife in the dark after those Masonic gatherings she turned away, with her potent disgust, from the smell of whisky on him. If the phylacteries and skull-cap were kept somewhere the children never saw them. He went fasting to the synagogue on the Day of Atonement and each year, on the anniversaries of the deaths of the old people in that village whom the wife and children had never seen, went again to light a candle. Feeble flame: who were they? In the quarrels between husband and wife, she saw them as ignorant and dirty; she must have read something somewhere that served as a taunt: you slept like animals round a stove, stinking of garlic, you bathed once a week. The children knew how low it was to be unwashed. And whipped into anger, he knew the lowest category of all in her country, this country.

You speak to me as if I was a kaffir.

The silence of cold countries at the approach of winter. On an island of mud, still standing where a village track parts like two locks of wet hair, a war memorial is crowned with the emblem of a lost occupying empire that has been succeeded by others, and still others. Under one or the other they lived, mending shoes and watches. Eating garlic and sleeping round the stove. In the graveyard stones lean against one another and sink at levels from one occupation and revolution to the next, the Zobos tick them off, the old woman shelling peas on the bench and the bearded man at the dockside are in mounds that are all cenotaphs because the script that records their names is a language he forgot and his daughters never knew. A burst of children out of school alights like pigeons round the monument. How is it possible that they cannot be understood as they stare, giggle and—the bold ones—question. As with the man in the train: from the tone, the expression on the faces, the curiosity, meaning is clear.

Who are you?

Where do you come from?

A map of Africa drawn with a stick in the mud.

Africa! The children punch each other and jig in recognition. They close in. One of them tugs at the gilt ring glinting in the ear of a little girl dark and hairy-curly as a poodle. They point: gold.

Those others knew about gold, long ago; for the poor and despised there is always the idea of gold somewhere else. That's why they packed him off when he was thirteen and according to their beliefs, a man.

At four in the afternoon the old moon bleeds radiance into the grey sky. In the wood a thick plumage of fallen oak leaves is laid reverentially as the feathers of the dead pheasants swinging from the beaters' belts. The beaters are coming across the great fields of maize in the first light of the moon. The guns probe its halo. Where I wait, apart, out of the way, hidden, I hear the rustle of fear among creatures. Their feathers swish against stalks and leaves. The clucking to gather in the young; the spurting squawks of terror as the men with their thrashing sticks drive the prey racing on, rushing this way and that, no way where there are not men and sticks, men and guns. They have wings but dare not fly and reveal themselves, there was nowhere to run to from the village to the fields as they came on and on, the kick of a cossack's mount ready to strike creeping heads, the thrust of a bayonet lifting a man by the heart like a piece of meat on a fork. Death advancing and nowhere to go. Blindness coming by fire or shot and no way out to see, shelling peas by feel. Cracks of detonation and wild agony of flutter all around me, I crouch away from the sound and sight, only a spectator, only a spectator, please, but the cossacks' hooves rode those pleading wretches down. A bird thuds dead, striking my shoulder before it hits the soft bed of leaves beside me.

Six leaves from my father's country.

When I began to know him, in his shop, as someone distinct from a lap I sat on, he shouted at the black man on the other side of the counter who swept the floor and ran errands, and he threw the man's weekly pay grudgingly at him. I saw there was someone my father had made afraid of him. A child understands fear, and the hurt and hate it brings.

I gathered the leaves for their pretty autumn stains, not out of any sentiment. This village where we've rented the State hunting lodge is not my father's village. I don't know where, in his country, it was, only the name of the port at which he left it behind. I didn't ask him about his village. He never told me; or I didn't listen. I have the leaves in my hand. I did not know that I would find, here in the wood, the beaters advancing, advancing across the world.

Some Are Born
to Sweet Delight

Some are Born to sweet delight,
Some are Born to Endless Night.

WILLIAM BLAKE—*'Auguries of Innocence'*

They took him in. Since their son had got himself signed up at sea for eighteen months on an oil rig, the boy's cubbyhole of a room was vacant; and the rent money was a help. There had rubbed off on the braid of the commissionaire father's uniform, through the contact of club members' coats and briefcases he relieved them of, loyal consciousness of the danger of bombs affixed under the cars of members of parliament and financiers. The father said 'I've no quarrel with that' when the owners of the house whose basement flat the family occupied stipulated 'No Irish'. But to discriminate against any other foreigners from the old Empire was against the principles of the house owners, who were also the mother's employers—cleaning three times a week and baby-sitting through the childhood of three boys she thought of as her own. So it was a way of pleasing Upstairs to let the room to this young man, a foreigner who likely had been turned away from other vacancies posted on a board at the supermarket. He was clean and tidy enough; and he didn't hang around the kitchen, hoping to be asked to eat with the family, the way one of their own kind would. He didn't eye Vera.

Vera was seventeen, and a filing clerk with prospects of advancement; her father had got her started in an important firm through the kindness of one of his gentlemen at the club. A word in the right place; and now it was up to her to become a secretary, maybe one day even a private secretary to someone like the members of the club, and travel to the Continent, America—anywhere.

—You have to dress decently for a firm like that. Let others show their backsides.—

—Dad!— The flat was small, the walls thin—suppose the lodger heard him. Her pupils dilated with a blush, half shyness, half annoyance. On Friday and Saturday nights she wore T-shirts with spangled graffiti across her breasts and went with girl-friends to the discothèque, although she'd had to let the pink side of her hair grow out. On Sundays they sat on wooden benches outside the pub with teasing local boys, drinking beer shandies. Once it was straight beer laced with something and they made her drunk, but her father had been engaged as doorman for a private party and her mother had taken the Upstairs children to the zoo, so nobody heard her vomiting in the bathroom.

So she thought.

He was in the kitchen when she went, wiping the slime from her panting mouth, to drink water. He always addressed her as 'miss'—Good afternoon, miss.— He was himself filling a glass.

She stopped where she was; sourness was in her mouth and nose, oozing towards the foreign stranger, she mustn't go a step nearer. Shame tingled over nausea and tears. Shame heaved in her stomach, her throat opened, and she just reached the sink in time to disgorge the final remains of a pizza minced by her teeth and digestive juices, floating in beer. —Go away. Go away!—her hand flung in rejection behind her. She opened both taps to blast her shame down the drain. —Get out!—

He was there beside her, in the disgusting stink of her, and he had wetted a dish-towel and was wiping her face, her dirty mouth, her tears. He was steadying her by the arm and sitting her down at the kitchen table. And she knew that his kind didn't even drink, he probably never had smelled alcohol before. If it had been one of her own crowd it would have been different.

She began to cry again. Very quietly, slowly, he put his hand on hers, taking charge of the wrist like a doctor preparing to follow the measure of a heart in a pulse-beat. Slowly—the pace was his—she quietened; she looked down, without moving her head, at the hand. Slowly, she drew her own hand from underneath, in parting.

As she left the kitchen a few meaningless echoes of what had happened to her went back and forth—are you all right yes I'm all right are you sure yes I'm all right.

She slept through her parents' return and next morning said she'd had flu.

He could no longer be an unnoticed presence in the house, outside her occupation with her work and the friends she made among the other junior employees, and her preoccupation, in her leisure, with the discothèque and cinema where the hand-holding and sex-tussles with local boys took place. He said, Good afternoon, as they saw each other approaching in the passage between the family's quarters and his room, or couldn't avoid coinciding at the gate of the tiny area garden where her mother's geraniums bloomed and the empty milk bottles were set out. He didn't say 'miss'; it was as if the omission were assuring, Don't worry, I won't tell anyone, *although I know all about what you do*, everything, I won't talk about you among my friends—did he even have any friends? Her mother told her he worked in the kitchens of a smart restaurant—her mother had to be sure a lodger had steady pay before he could be let into the house. Vera saw other foreigners like him about, gathered loosely as if they didn't know where to go; of course, they didn't come to the disco and they were not part of the crowd of familiars at the cinema. They were together but looked alone. It was something noticed the way she might notice, without expecting to fathom, the strange expression of a caged animal, far from wherever it belonged.

She owed him a signal in return for his trustworthiness. Next time they happened to meet in the house she said —I'm Vera.—

As if he didn't know, hadn't heard her mother and father call her. Again he did the right thing, merely nodded politely.

—I've never really caught your name.—

—Our names are hard for you, here. Just call me Rad.— His English was stiff, pronounced syllable by syllable in a soft voice.

—So it's short for something?—

—What is that?—

—A nickname. Bob for Robert.—

—Something like that.—

She ended this first meeting on a new footing the only way she knew how: —Well, see you later, then—the vague dismissal used casually among her friends when no such commitment existed. But on a Sunday when she was leaving the house to wander down to see who was gathered at the pub she went up the basement steps and saw that he was in the area garden. He was reading newspapers—three or four of them stacked on the mud-plastered grass at his side. She picked up his name and used it for the first time, easily as a key turning in a greased lock. —Hullo, Rad.—

He rose from the chair he had brought out from his room. —I hope your mother won't mind? I wanted to ask, but she's not at home.—

—Oh no, not Ma, we've had that old chair for ages, a bit of fresh air won't crack it up more than it is already.—

She stood on the short path, he stood beside the old rattan chair; then sat down again so that she could walk off without giving offence—she left to her friends, he left to his reading.

She said—I won't tell.—

And so it was out, what was between them alone, in the family house. And they laughed, smiled, both of them. She walked over to where he sat. —Got the day off? You work in some restaurant, don't you, what's it like?—

—I'm on the evening shift today.— He stayed himself a moment, head on one side, with aloof boredom. —It's something. Just a job. What you can get.—

—I know. But I suppose working in a restaurant at least the food's thrown in, as well.—

He looked out over the railings a moment, away from her. —I don't eat that food.—

She began to be overcome by a strong reluctance to go through the gate, round the corner, down the road to The Mitre and the whistles and appreciative pinches which would greet her in her new flowered Bermudas, his black eyes following her all the way, although he'd be reading his papers with her forgotten. To gain time she looked at the papers. The one in his hand was English. On the others, lying there, she was confronted with a flowing script of tails and gliding flourishes, the secret of somebody else's language. She could not go to the pub; she could not let him know that was where she was going. The deceptions that did for parents were not for him. But the fact was there was no deception: she *wasn't* going to the pub, she suddenly wasn't going.

She sat down on the motoring section of the English newspaper he'd discarded and crossed her legs in an X from the bare round knees. —Good news from home?—

He gestured with his foot towards the papers in his secret language; his naked foot was an intimate object, another secret.

—From my home, no good news.—

She understood this must be some business about politics, over there—she was in awe and ignorance of politics, nothing to do with her. —So that's why you went away.—

He didn't need to answer.

—You know, I can't imagine going away.—

—You don't want to leave your friends.—

She caught the allusion, pulled a childish face, dismissing them. —Mum and Dad . . . everything.—

He nodded, as if in sympathy for her imagined loss, but made no admission of what must be his own.

—Though I'm mad keen to travel. I mean, that's my idea, taking this job. Seeing other places—just visiting, you know. If I make myself capable and that, I might get the chance. There's one secretary in our offices who goes everywhere with her boss, she brings us all back souvenirs, she's very generous.—

—You want to see the world. But now your friends are waiting for you—

She shook off the insistence with a laugh. —And you want to go home!—

—No.— He looked at her with the distant expression of an adult before the innocence of a child. —Not yet.—

The authority of his mood over hers, that had been established in the kitchen that time, was there. She was hesitant and humble rather than flirtatious when she changed the subject. —Shall we have—will you have some tea if I make it? Is it all right?— He'd never eaten in the house; perhaps the family's food and drink were taboo for him in his religion, like the stuff he could have eaten free in the restaurant.

He smiled. —Yes it's all right.— And he got up and padded along behind her on his slim feet to the kitchen. As with a wipe over the clean surfaces of her mother's sink and table, the other time in the kitchen was cleared by ordinary business about brewing tea, putting out cups. She set him to cut the gingerbread: —Go on, try it, it's my mother's homemade.— She watched with an anxious smile, curiosity, while his beautiful teeth broke into its crumbling softness. He nodded, granting grave approval with a full mouth. She mimicked him, nodding and smiling; and, like a doe approaching a leaf, she took from his hand the fragrant slice with the semicircle marked by his teeth, and took a bite out of it.

Vera didn't go to the pub any more. At first they came to look for her—her chums, her mates—and nobody believed her excuses when she wouldn't come along with them. She hung about the house on Sundays, helping her mother. —Have you had a tiff or something?—

As she always told her bosom friends, she was lucky with her kind of mother, not strict and suspicious like some. —No, Ma. They're okay, but it's always the same thing, same things to say, every weekend.—

—Well . . . shows you're growing up, moving on—it's natural. You'll find new friends, more interesting, more your type.—

Vera listened to hear if he was in his room or had had to go to work—his shifts at the restaurant, she had learnt from timing his presence and absences, were irregular. He was very quiet, didn't play a radio or cassettes but she always could feel if he was there, in his room. That summer was a real summer for once; if he was off shift he would bring the old rattan chair into the garden and read, or stretch out his legs and lie back with his face lifted to the humid sun. He must be thinking of where he came from; very hot, she imagined it, desert and thickly-white cubes of houses with palm trees. She went out with a rug—nothing unusual about wanting to sunbathe in your own area garden—and chatted to him as if just because he happened to be there. She watched his eyes travelling from right to left along the scrolling print of his newspapers, and when he paused, yawned, rested his head and closed his lids against the light, could ask him about home—his home. He described streets and cities and cafés and bazaars—it wasn't at all like her idea of desert and oases. —But there are palm trees?—

—Yes, nightclubs, rich people's palaces to show tourists, but there are also factories and prison camps and poor people living on a handful of beans a day.—

She picked at the grass: I see. —Were you—were your family—do you like beans?—

He was not to be drawn; he was never to be drawn.

—If you know how to make them, they are good.—

—If we get some, will you tell us how they're cooked?—

—I'll make them for you.—

So one Sunday Vera told her mother Rad, the lodger, wanted to prepare a meal for the family. Her parents were rather touched; nice, here was a delicate mark of gratitude, such a glum character, he'd never shown any sign before. Her father was prepared to put up with something that probably wouldn't agree with him. —Different people, different ways. Maybe it's a custom with them, when they're taken in, like bringing a bunch of flowers.— The meal went off well. The dish was delicious and not too spicy; after all, gingerbread was spiced, too. When her father opened a bottle of beer and put it down at Rad's place, Vera quickly lifted it away. —He doesn't drink, Dad.—

Graciousness called forth graciousness; Vera's mother issued a reciprocal invitation. —You must come and have our Sunday dinner one day—my chicken with apple pie to follow.—

But the invitation was in the same code as 'See you later'. It was not mentioned again. One Sunday Vera shook the grass from her rug. —I'm going for a walk.— And the lodger slowly got up from his chair, put his newspaper aside, and they went through the gate. The neighbours must have seen her with him. The pair went where she led, although they were side by side, loosely, the way she'd seen young men of his kind together. They went on walking a long way, down streets and then into a park. She loved to watch people flying kites; now he was the one who watched her as she watched. It seemed to be his way of getting to know her; to know anything. It wasn't the way of other boys—her kind—but then he was a foreigner here, there must be so much he needed to find out. Another weekend she had the idea to take a picnic. That meant an outing for the whole day. She packed apples and bread and cheese—remembering no ham—under the eyes of her mother. There was a silence between them. In it was her mother's recognition of the accusation she, Vera, knew she ought to bring against herself: Vera was 'chasing' a man; this man. All her mother said was—Are you joining other friends?— She didn't lie. —No. He's never been up the river. I thought we'd take a boat trip.—

In time she began to miss the cinema. Without guile she asked him if he had seen this film or that; she presumed that when he was heard going out for the evening the cinema would be where he went, with friends of his—his kind—she never saw. What did they do if they didn't go to a movie? It wouldn't be bars, and she knew instinctively he wouldn't be found in a disco, she couldn't see him shaking and stomping under twitching coloured lights.

He hadn't seen any film she mentioned. —Won't you come?— It happened like the first walk. He looked at her again as he had then. —D'you think so?—

—Why ever not. Everybody goes to movies.—

But she knew why not. She sat beside him in the theatre with solemnity. It was unlike any other time, in that familiar place of pleasure. He did not hold her hand; only that time, that time in the kitchen. They went together to the cinema regularly. The silence between her and her parents grew; her mother was like a cheerful bird whose cage had been covered. Whatever her mother and father thought, whatever they feared—nothing had happened, nothing happened until one public holiday when Vera and the lodger were both off work and they went on one of their long walks into the country (that was all they could do, he didn't play sport, there wasn't any activity with other young people he knew how to enjoy). On that day celebrated for a royal birthday or religious anniversary that couldn't mean anything to him, in deep grass under profound trees he made love to Vera for the first time. He had never so much as kissed her, before, not on any evening walking home from the cinema, not when they were alone in the house and the opportunity was obvious as the discretion of the kitchen clock sounding through the empty passage, and the blind eye of the television set in the sitting-room. All that he had never done with her was begun and accomplished with unstoppable passion, summoned up as if at a mere command to himself; between this and the placing of his hand on hers in the kitchen, months before, there was nothing. Now she had the lips from which, like a doe, she had taken a morsel touched with his saliva, she had the naked body promised by the first glimpse of the naked feet. She had lost her virginity, like all her sister schoolgirls, at fourteen or fifteen, she had been fucked, half-struggling, by some awkward local in a car or a back room, once or twice. But now she was overcome, amazed, engulfed by a sensuality she had no idea was inside her, a bounty of talent unexpected and unknown as a burst of song would have been welling from one who knew she had no voice. She wept with love for this man who might never, never have come to her, never have found her from so far away. She wept because she was so afraid it might so nearly never have happened. He wiped her tears, he dressed her with the comforting resignation to her emotion a mother shows with an over-excited child.

She didn't hope to conceal from her mother what they were doing; she knew her mother knew. Her mother felt her gliding silently from her room down the passage to the lodger's room, the room that still smelt of her brother, late at night, and returning very early in the morning. In the dark Vera knew every floorboard that creaked, how to avoid the swish of her pyjamas touching past a wall; at dawn saw the squinting beam of the rising sun sloped through a window that she had never known was so placed it could let in any phase of the sun's passage across the sky. Everything was changed.

What could her mother have said? Maybe he had different words in his language; the only ones she and her mother had wouldn't do, weren't meant for a situation not provided for in their lives. *Do you know what you're doing? Do you know what he is? We don't have any objection to them, but all the same. What about your life? What about the good firm your father's got you into? What'll it look like, there?*

The innocent release of sensuality in the girl gave her an authority that prevailed in the house. She brought him to the table for meals, now; he ate what he could. Her parents knew this presence, in the code of their kind, only as the signal by which an 'engaged' daughter would bring home her intended. But outwardly between Vera and her father and mother the form was kept up that his position was still that of a lodger, a lodger who had somehow become part of the household in that capacity. There was no need for him to pretend or assume any role; he never showed any kind of presumption towards their daughter, spoke to her with the same reserve that he, a stranger, showed to them. When he and the girl rose from the table to go out together it was always as if he accompanied her, without interest, at her volition.

Because her father was a man, even if an old one and her father, he recognized the power of sensuality in a female and was defeated, intimidated by its obstinacy. *He* couldn't take the whole business up with her; her mother must do that. He quarrelled with his wife over it. So she confronted their daughter. *Where will it end?* Both she and the girl understood: he'll go back where he comes from, and where'll you be? He'll drop you when he's had enough of what he wanted from you.

Where would it end? Rad occasionally acknowledged her among his friends, now—it turned out he did have some friends, yes, young men like him, from his home. He and she encountered them on the street and instead of excusing himself and leaving her waiting obediently like one of those pet dogs tied up outside the supermarket, as he usually had done when he went over to speak to his friends, he took her with him and, as if remembering her presence after a minute or two of talk, interrupted himself: She's Vera. Their greetings, the way they looked at her, made her feel that he had told them about her, after all, and she was happy. They made remarks in their own language she was sure referred to her. If she had moved on, from the pub, the disco, the parents, she was accepted, belonged somewhere else.

And then she found she was pregnant. She had no girl-friend to turn to who could be trusted not to say those things: he'll go back where he comes from he'll drop you when he's had enough of what he wanted from you. After the second month she bought a kit from the pharmacy and tested her urine. Then she went to a doctor because that do-it-yourself thing might be mistaken.

—I thought you said you would be all right.—

That was all he said, after thinking for a moment, when she told him.

—Don't worry, I'll find something. I'll do something about it. I'm sorry, Rad. Just forget it.— She was afraid he would stop loving her—her term for love-making.

When she went to him tentatively that night he caressed her more beautifully and earnestly than ever while possessing her.

She remembered reading in some women's magazine that it was dangerous to do anything to get rid of 'it' (she gave her pregnancy no other identity) after three months. Through roundabout enquiries she found a doctor who did abortions, and booked an appointment, taking an advance on her holiday bonus to meet the fee asked.

—By the way, it'll be all over next Saturday. I've found someone.— Timidly, that week, she brought up the subject she had avoided between them.

He looked at her as if thinking very carefully before he spoke, thinking apart from her, in his own language, as she was often sure he was doing. Perhaps he had forgotten— it was really her business, her fault, she knew. Then he pronounced what neither had: —The baby?—

—Well . . .— She waited, granting this.

He did not take her in his arms, he did not touch her. —You will have the baby. We will marry.—

It flew from her awkward, unbelieving, aghast with joy: —You want to marry me!—

—Yes, you're going to be my wife.—

—Because of this?—a baby?—

He was gazing at her intensely, wandering over the sight of her. —Because I've chosen you.—

Of course, being a foreigner, he didn't come out with things the way an English speaker would express them.

And I love *you*, she said, I love you, I love you—babbling through vows and tears. He put a hand on one of hers, as he had done in the kitchen of her mother's house; once, and never since.

She saw a couple in a mini-series standing hand-in-hand, telling them; 'We're getting married'—hugs and laughter.

But she told her parents alone, without him there. It was safer that way, she thought, for him. And she phrased it in proof of his good intentions as a triumphant answer to her mother's warnings, spoken and unspoken. —Rad's going to marry me.—

—He wants to marry you?— Her mother corrected. The burst of a high-pitched cry. The father twitched an angry look at his wife.

Now it was time for the scene to conform to the TV family announcement. —We're going to get married.—

Her father's head flew up and sank slowly, he turned away.

—You want to be married to him?— Her mother's palm spread on her breast to cover the blow.

The girl was brimming feeling, reaching for them.

Her father was shaking his head like a sick dog.

—And I'm pregnant and he's glad.—

Her mother turned to her father but there was no help coming from him. She spoke impatiently flatly. —So that's it.—

—No, that's not it. It's not it at all.— She would not say to them 'I love him', she would not let them spoil that by trying to make her feel ashamed. —It's what I want.—

—It's what she wants.— Her mother was addressing her father.

He had to speak. He gestured towards his daughter's body, where there was no sign yet to show life growing there. —Nothing to be done then.—

When the girl had left the room he glared at his wife. —Bloody bastard.—

—Hush. Hush.— There was a baby to be born, poor innocent.

And it was, indeed, the new life the father had gestured at in Vera's belly that changed everything. The foreigner, the lodger—had to think of him now as the future son-in-law, Vera's intended—told Vera and her parents he was sending her to his home for his parents to meet her. —To your country?—

He answered with the gravity with which, they realized, marriage was regarded where he came from. —The bride must meet the parents. They must know her as I know hers.—

If anyone had doubted the seriousness of his intentions— well, they could be ashamed of those doubts, now; he was sending her home, openly and proudly, his foreigner, to be accepted by his parents. —But have you told them about the baby, Rad?— She didn't express this embarrassment in front of her mother and father. —What do you think? That is why you are going.— He slowed, then spoke again. —It's a child of our family.—

So she was going to travel at last! In addition to every other joy! In a state of continual excitement between desire for Rad—now openly sharing her room with her—and the pride of telling her work-mates why she was taking her annual leave just then, she went out of her way to encounter former friends whom she had avoided. To say she was travelling to meet her fiancé's family; she was getting married in a few months, she was having a baby—yes—proof of this now in the rounding under the flowered jumpsuit she wore to show it off. For her mother, too, a son-in-law who was not one of their kind became a distinction rather than a shame. —Our Vera's a girl who's always known her own mind. It's a changing world, she's not one just to go on repeating the same life as we've had.— The only thing that hadn't changed in the world was joy over a little one coming. Vera was thrilled, they were all thrilled at the idea of a baby, a first grandchild. Oh that one was going to be spoilt all right! The prospective grandmother was knitting, although Vera laughed and said babies weren't dressed in that sort of thing any more, hers was going to wear those little unisex frog suits in bright colours. There was a deposit down on a pram fit for an infant prince or princess.

It was understood that if the intended could afford to send his girl all the way home just to meet his parents before the wedding, he had advanced himself in the restaurant business, despite the disadvantages young men like him had in an unwelcoming country. Upstairs was pleased with the news; Upstairs came down one evening and brought a bottle of champagne as a gift to toast Vera, whom they'd known since she was a child, and her boy—much pleasant laughter when the prospective husband filled everyone's glass and then served himself with orange juice. Even the commissionaire felt confident enough to tell one of his gentlemen at the club that his daughter was getting married, but first about to go abroad to meet the young man's parents. His gentlemen's children were always travelling; in his ears every day were overheard snatches of destinations—'by bicycle in China, can you believe it'...'two months in Peru, rather nice...'...'snorkeling on the Barrier Reef, last I heard'. *Visiting her future parents-in-law where there is desert and palm trees*; not bad!

The parents wanted to have a little party, before she left, a combined engagement party and farewell. Vera had in mind a few of her old friends brought together with those friends of his she'd been introduced to and with whom she knew he still spent some time—she didn't expect to go along with him, it wasn't their custom for women, and she couldn't understand their language, anyway. But he didn't seem to think a party would work. She had her holiday bonus (to remember what she had drawn it for, originally, was something that, feeling the baby tapping its presence softly inside her, she couldn't believe of herself) and she kept asking him what she could buy as presents for his family—his parents, his sisters and brothers, she had learnt all their names. He said he would buy things, he knew what to get. As the day for her departure approached, he still had not done so. —But I want to pack! I want to know how much room to leave, Rad!— He brought some men's clothing she couldn't judge and some dresses and scarves she didn't like but didn't dare say so—she supposed the clothes his sisters liked were quite different from what she enjoyed wearing—a good thing she hadn't done the choosing.

She didn't want her mother to come to the airport; they'd both be too emotional. Leaving Rad was strangely different; it was not leaving Rad but going, carrying his baby, to the mystery that was Rad, that was in Rad's silences, his blind love-making, the way he watched her, thinking in his own language so that she could not follow anything in his eyes.

It would all be revealed when she arrived where he came from.

He had to work, the day she left, until it was time to take her to the airport. Two of his friends, whom she could scarcely recognize from the others in the group she had met occasionally, came with him to fetch her in the taxi one of them drove. She held Rad's hand, making a tight double fist on his thigh, while the men talked in their language. At the airport the others left him to go in alone with her. He gave her another, last-minute gift for home. —Oh Rad— where'm I going to put it? The ticket says one hand-baggage!— But she squeezed his arm in happy recognition of his thoughts for his family. —It can go in—easy, easy.— He unzipped her carryall as they stood in the queue at the check-in counter. She knelt with her knees spread to accommodate her belly, and helped him. —What is it, any-way—I hope not something that's going to break?— He was making a bed for the package. —Just toys for my sister's kid. Plastic.— —I could have put them in the suitcase—oh Rad . . . what room'll I have for duty-free!— In her excite-ment, she was addressing the queue for the American air-line's flight which would take her on the first leg of her journey. These fellow passengers were another kind of for-eigner, Americans, but she felt she knew them all; they were going to be travelling in her happiness, she was taking them with her.

She held him with all her strength and he kept her pressed against his body; she could not see his face. He stood and watched her as she went through passport control and she stopped again and again to wave but she saw Rad could not wave, could not wave. Only watch her until he could not see her any longer. And she saw him in her mind, still looking at her, as she had done at the beginning when she had imagined herself as still under his eyes if she had gone to the pub on a Sunday morning.

Over the sea, the airliner blew up in midair. Everyone on board died. The black box was recovered from the bed of the sea and revealed that there had been an explosion in the tourist-class cabin followed by a fire; and there the messages ended; silence, the disintegration of the plane. No one knows if all were killed outright or if some survived to drown. An inquiry into the disaster continued for a year. The background of every passenger was traced, and the circumstances that led to the journey of each. There were some arrests; people detained for questioning and then released. They were innocent—but they were foreigners, of course. Then there was another disaster of the same nature, and a statement from a group with an apocalyptic name representing a faction of the world's wronged, claiming the destruction of both planes in some complication of vengeance for holy wars, land annexation, invasions, imprisonments, cross-border raids, territorial disputes, bombings, sinkings, kidnappings no one outside the initiated could understand. A member of the group, a young man known as Rad among many other aliases, had placed in the handbaggage of the daughter of the family with whom he lodged, and who was pregnant by him, an explosive device. Plastic. A bomb of a plastic type undetectable by the usual procedures of airport security.

Vera was chosen.

Vera had taken them all, taken the baby inside her; down, along with her happiness.

Comrades

As Mrs. Hattie Telford pressed the electronic gadget that deactivates the alarm device in her car a group of youngsters came up behind her. Black. But no need to be afraid; this was not a city street. This was a non-racial enclave of learning, a place where tended flowerbeds and trees bearing botanical identification plates civilized the wild reminder of campus guards and dogs. The youngsters, like her, were part of the crowd loosening into dispersion after a university conference on People's Education. They were the people to be educated; she was one of the committee of white and black activists (convenient generic for revolutionaries, leftists secular and Christian, fellow-travellers and liberals) up on the platform.

—Comrade... — She was settling in the driver's seat when one so slight and slim he seemed a figure in profile came up to her window. He drew courage from the friendly lift of the woman's eyebrows above blue eyes, the tilt of her freckled white face: —Comrade, are you going to town?—

No, she was going in the opposite direction, home . . . but quickly, in the spirit of the hall where these young people had been somewhere, somehow present with her (ah no, she with them) stamping and singing Freedom songs, she would take them to the bus station their spokesman named. —Climb aboard!—

The others got in the back, the spokesman beside her. She saw the nervous white of his eyes as he glanced at and away from her. She searched for talk to set them at ease. Questions, of course. Older people always start with questioning young ones. Did they come from Soweto?

They came from Harrismith, Phoneng Location.

She made the calculation: about two hundred kilometres distant. How did they get here? Who told them about the conference?

—We are Youth Congress in Phoneng.—

A delegation. They had come by bus; one of the groups and stragglers who kept arriving long after the conference had started. They had missed, then, the free lunch?

At the back, no one seemed even to be breathing. The spokesman must have had some silent communication with them, some obligation to speak for them created by the journey or by other shared experience in the mysterious bonds of the young—these young. —We are hungry.— And from the back seats was drawn an assent like the suction of air in a compressing silence.

She was silent in response, for the beat of a breath or two. These large gatherings both excited and left her overexposed, open and vulnerable to the rub and twitch of the mass shuffling across rows of seats and loping up the aisles, babies' fudge-brown soft legs waving as their napkins are changed on mothers' laps, little girls with plaited loops on their heads listening like old crones, heavy women swaying to chants, men with fierce, unreadably black faces breaking into harmony tender and deep as they sing to God for his protection of Umkhonto weSizwe, as people on both sides have always, everywhere, claimed divine protection for their soldiers, their wars. At the end of a day like this she wanted a drink, she wanted the depraved luxury of solitude and quiet in which she would be restored (enriched, oh yes! by the day) to the familiar limits of her own being.

Hungry. Not for iced whisky and feet up. It seemed she had scarcely hesitated: —Look, I live nearby, come back to my house and have something to eat. Then I'll run you into town.—

—That will be very nice. We can be glad for that.— And at the back the tight vacuum relaxed.

They followed her in through the gate, shrinking away from the dog—she assured them he was harmless but he was large, with a fancy collar by which she held him. She trooped them in through the kitchen because that was the way she always entered her house, something she would not have done if they had been adult, her black friends whose sophistication might lead them to believe the choice of entrance was an unthinking historical slight. As she was going to feed them, she took them not into her living-room with its sofas and flowers but into her dining-room, so that they could sit at table right away. It was a room in confident taste that could afford to be spare: bare floorboards, matching golden wooden ceiling, antique brass chandelier, reed blinds instead of stuffy curtains. An African wooden sculpture represented a lion marvellously released from its matrix in the grain of a Mukwa tree-trunk. She pulled up the chairs and left the four young men while she went back to the

kitchen to make coffee and see what there was in the refrigerator for sandwiches. They had greeted the maid, in
the language she and they shared, on their way through
the kitchen, but when the maid and the lady of the house
had finished preparing cold meat and bread, and the coffee
was ready, she suddenly did not want them to see that the
maid waited on her. She herself carried the heavy tray into
the dining-room.

They are sitting round the table, silent, and there is no
impression that they stopped an undertone exchange when
they heard her approaching. She doles out plates, cups.
They stare at the food but their eyes seem focused on something she can't see; something that overwhelms. She urges
them—Just cold meat, I'm afraid, but there's chutney if you
like it...milk everybody?...is the coffee too strong, I have
a heavy hand, I know. Would anyone like to add some hot
water?—
They eat. When she tries to talk to one of the others, he
says *Ekskuus?* And she realizes he doesn't understand English, of the white man's languages knows perhaps only a
little of that of the Afrikaners in the rural town he comes
from. Another gives his name, as if in some delicate acknowledgement of the food. —I'm Shadrack Nsutsha.—
She repeats the surname to get it right. But he does not
speak again. There is an urgent exchange of eye-language,
and the spokesman holds out the emptied sugar-bowl to
her. —Please.— She hurries to the kitchen and brings it
back refilled. They need carbohydrate, they are hungry,
they are young, they need it, they burn it up. She is dis-
tressed at the inadequacy of the meal and then notices the

fruit bowl, her big copper fruit bowl, filled with apples and bananas and perhaps there is a peach or two under the grape leaves with which she likes to complete an edible still life. —Have some fruit. Help yourselves.—

They are stacking their plates and cups, not knowing what they are expected to do with them in this room which is a room where apparently people only eat, do not cook, do not sleep. While they finish the bananas and apples (Shadrack Nsutsha had seen the single peach and quickly got there first) she talks to the spokesman, whose name she has asked for: Dumile. —Are you still at school, Dumile?— Of course he is not at school—*they* are not at school; youngsters their age have not been at school for several years, they are the children growing into young men and women for whom school is a battleground, a place of boycotts and demonstrations, the literacy of political rhetoric, the education of revolt against having to live the life their parents live. They have pompous titles of responsibility beyond childhood: he is chairman of his branch of the Youth Congress, he was expelled two years ago—for leading a boycott? Throwing stones at the police? Maybe burning the school down? He calls it all—quietly, abstractly, doesn't know many ordinary, concrete words but knows these euphemisms—'political activity'. No school for two years? No. —So what have you been able to do with yourself, all that time?—

She isn't giving him a chance to eat his apple. He swallows a large bite, shaking his head on its thin, little-boy neck. —I was inside. Detained from this June for six months.—

She looks round the others. —And you?—

Shadrack seems to nod slightly. The other two look at her. She should know, she should have known, it's a common enough answer from youths like them, their colour. They're not going to be saying they've been selected for the 1st Eleven at cricket or that they're off on a student tour to Europe in the school holidays.

The spokesman, Dumile, tells her he wants to study by correspondence, 'get his matric' that he was preparing for two years ago; two years ago when he was still a child, when he didn't have the hair that is now appearing on his face, making him a man, taking away the childhood. In the hesitations, the silences of the table, where there is nervously spilt coffee among plates of banana skins, there grows the certainty that he will never get the papers filled in for the correspondence college, he will never get the two years back. She looks at them all and cannot believe what she knows: that they, suddenly here in her house, will carry the AK-47s they only sing about, now, miming death as they sing. They will have a career of wiring explosives to the undersides of vehicles, they will go away and come back through the bush to dig holes not to plant trees to shade home, but to plant land-mines. She can see they have been terribly harmed but cannot believe they could harm. They are wiping their fruit-sticky hands furtively palm against palm.

She breaks the silence; says something, anything.

—How d'you like my lion? Isn't he beautiful? He's made by a Zimbabwean artist, I think the name's Dube.—

But the foolish interruption becomes revelation. Dumile, in his gaze—distant, lingering, speechless this time—reveals what has overwhelmed them. In this room, the space, the expensive antique chandelier, the consciously simple choice of reed blinds, the carved lion: all are on the same level of impact, phenomena undifferentiated, undecipherable. Only the food that fed their hunger was real.

Teraloyna

A place for goats—we all must leave.

Othello called here.

That's all it was fit for, our island. The goats. After how
long we don't know; because we don't know how or when
we got there: a shipwreck must have started us, we have
one family name only—Teraloyna. But Othello stopped
here; they came over in small boats, black men with
spears. They did not harm us. We had always fished with
nets woven of bark; they taught us to spear the great fish
who broke our nets. They never went back wherever it was
they came from. And so when we left we had among us
only a child here and there who was raw-faced and blue-
eyed; we were coloured neither very dark nor very light.

We don't know how the goats came. Perhaps there was a pair of goats on board, for the milk, and they swam ashore from the wreck. Ours were strong, large goats, they had a great many young. They had many more young than we had; in the end they ate up the island—the grass, the trees, at night in our houses we could hear those long front teeth of theirs, paring it away. When the rains came our soil had nothing to hold it, although we made terraces of stones. It washed away and disappeared into the shining sea. We killed and ate a lot of goats but they occupied some parts of the island where we couldn't get at them with our ropes and knives, and every year there were more of them. Someone remembered us—a sailor's tale of people who had never seen the mainland of the world?—and we were recruited. We took our grandmothers and the survivors of our matings of father and daughter, brother and sister (we never allowed matings of mother and son, we were Christians in our way, in custom brought down to us from the shipwreck) and we emigrated to these great open lands—America, Australia, Africa. We cleaned the streets and dug the dams and begged and stole; became like anybody else. The children forgot the last few words of the shipwreck dialect we once had spoken. Our girls married and no longer bore our name. In time we went into the armies, we manned the street stands selling ice-cream and hot dogs, all over the mainland that is the world.

The goats died of famine. They were able to swim to survival from a ship, but not across an ocean. Vegetation and wildlife, altered forever by erosion, crept back: blade by blade, footprint by footprint. Sea-birds screamed instead of human infants. The island was nevertheless a possession; handed out among the leftovers in the disposition of territories made by victors in one or other of the great wars waged on the mainland. But neither the United States nor Britain, nor the Soviet Union, was interested in it; useless, from the point of view of its position, for defence of any sea-route. Then meteorologists of the country to which it had been given found that position ideal for a weather station. It has been successfully manned for many years by teams of meteorologists who, at first, made the long journey by ship, and more recently and conveniently by plane.

A team's tour of duty on the island is a year, during which the shine of the sea blinds them to the mainland as it did those who once inhabited the island. A long year. A plane brings supplies every month, and there is communication by radio, but—with the exception of the goats, the islanders must have kept goats, there are the bones of goats everywhere—the team has neither more nor less company than the islanders had. Of course, these are educated people, scientists, and there is a reasonable library and taped music; even whole plays recorded, someone in one of the teams left behind cassettes of Gielgud's Lear and Olivier's Othello—there is a legend that Othello was blown in to anchor at the island. The personnel are subject to the same pests the original inhabitants suffered—ticks, mosquitoes, recurrent plagues of small mice. Supposedly to eat the mice, but maybe (by default of the softness of a woman?) to have something warm to stroke while the winter gales try to drown the weather station in the sea that cuts it adrift from humankind, a member of a team brought two kittens with him from the mainland on his tour of duty. They slept in his bed for a year. They were fed tit-bits by everyone at that table so far from any other at which people gather for an evening meal.

The island is not near anywhere. But as it is nearest to Africa, when the islanders left towards the end of the last century, some went there. Already there were mines down in the south of the continent and the communities of strangers diamonds and gold attract; not only miners, but boardinghouse- bar- and brothel-keepers, shopkeepers and tradesmen. So most of the islanders who went to Africa were shipped to the south and, without skills other than fishnet-making and herding goats—which were redundant, since commercially-produced nets were available to the fishing fleets manned by people of mixed white, Malay, Indian and Khoikhoi blood, and only the blacks, who minded their own flocks, kept goats—they found humble work among these communities. Exogamous marriage made their descendants' hair frizzier or straighter, their skin darker or lighter, depending on whether they attached themselves in this way to black people, white people, or those already singled out and named as partly both. The raw-faced, blue-eyed ones, of course, disappeared among the whites; and sometimes shaded back, in the next generation, to a darker colour and category—already there were categories, laws that decreed what colour and degree of colour could live where. The islanders who were absorbed into the darker-skinned communities became the Khans and Abramses and Kuzwayos, those who threaded away among the generations of whites became the Bezuidenhouts, Cloetes, Labuschagnes and even the Churches, Taylors and Smiths.

The Teraloynas are an obscure curiosity in the footnotes of ethnologists. The surname survives here and there; the people who bear it are commonly thought, without any evidence but a vague matching of vowel sounds, to be of Spanish or Portuguese origin. Linguists interested in the distortion of proper names in multilingual, colonized countries have suggested the name probably derives from a pidgin contraction of two words the shipwrecked, presumably French-speaking, used to describe where they found themselves. 'Terre'—earth, 'loin'—far: the far earth.

The Teraloynas occupy no twig on the family trees of white people. Whites in that country have not yet acquired the far-sighted circumspection of claiming a trace of black in their genes, and blacks who, in pride of origin and search for unity among their different shades of black, claim an admixture of the blood of non-negroid indigenes, the Khoikhoi and San, never bother to assert kinship with such scarcely-identifiable bastard groups as the St. Helenans (Napoleon had a forced stay on their island) or the Teraloynas. Those of Teraloyna descent whose blood is so diluted that no one—least of all themselves—could learn from the shape of their mouths and noses, the lie of their hair, from their names or habits of speech that they have such ancestry, sometimes fly in Business Class over their island: down there, all wrinkled and pleated in erosion, all folds (the ravines where the goats held out so long) and dark inlets edged at the mouth by the spittle of the sea—it is not marked on the coloured route map in the flight magazine provided in each seat-pocket. Their island; and they emigrated from that unrecognized piece of earth, poked up out of the sea, to the great open lands—America, Australia, Africa. They doze in their seats.

When a certain black carpenter draws a splinter from under his nail, the bubble of blood that comes after it is Teraloyna. And when a certain young white man, drafted into military service straight from school, throws a canister of tear-gas into a schoolyard full of black children and is hit on the cheek by a cast stone, the broken capillaries ooze Teraloyna lifeblood.

It is a mere graze, he is lucky, he might have lost a blue eye.

This year there are six hundred cats on the island. An estimate: there may be many more, they breed in the ravines. Their mating howls sound terrifyingly over the night sea. Othello would turn about in horror from an island of demons. Survivors from a wreck would rather go under than make for that other death.

But they are really only cats—the demons. Descendants of two kittens, a pretty black queen with a beauty patch of white on her cheek and a ginger tabby tom, who kneaded the pillows of a member of one of the meteorological teams in his lonely nights and were fed tit-bits at the only dining table for thousands of sea-miles around.

The meteorologists have tried poisoned meat, and being scientifically-minded, infection with cat flu, so deadly to pets on any mainland. But these feral creatures know no mainland. The soft beds and tit-bits have disappeared in ancestral memory. They have forgotten the comforts and dependence on humans natural to them; to succumb to the forms of eradication devised by humans would be a form of atavism. Their howls are the only cries heard on the island; they have eaten all the eggs of the sea-birds. They have caused the giant turtles to disobey, in amphibian wisdom, the imperative of their slow drag up the beaches to lay their eggs; the turtles have learnt something they did not need to know before in thousands of years in the chain of their existence: that cats, the claws of cats will dig up their eggs no matter how much breath—and how agonizing it is to breathe, out of water!—is expended in burying them in the sand. The hares are fast being eaten out; and even the butterflies—caterpillars are milky-bodied and nutritious.

The meteorologists have no trouble with mice, of course. But two kittens, so soft and small, have almost destroyed the ecology of the island, and this (apart from the infernal wails of feline rut) is an embarrassment to the team. When the SPCA protests against the cruelty of inflicting on animals a painful death by germ warfare, the meteorologists cite the near-extinction, by those non-indigenous animals, of wildlife. But this only emphasizes the careless disregard for ecological balance shown in the first place; why were the kittens not spayed, in the case of the female, and castrated, in the case of the male (a precaution against his mating with some kind of wild feline that might have existed on the island)? Well, they were pets, and nobody thought of it, nobody could have dreamt of the consequences: of such fierce fecundity in that place where there were no women. It was simply out of mind; out of the mainland.

A new solution is to be tried.

The fact is, there is an emergency on the island.

As the solution involves an element of sportsmanship— who could be persuaded to carry it out, otherwise?—it was never intended to get into the papers, but due to another indiscretion on somebody's part, it has. Only a line or two: the cats are to be shot. If the hunters are good marksmen the death will be far quicker and less painful than death by arsenic or cat flu. The meteorologists are not the sort of men who shoot for sport, of course, they don't handle firearms, so others must be found to do it. The army would be the obvious choice, but another sort of State of Emergency exists in the mainland country and all troops are required to man the borders, take part in pre-emptive raids across them, and install themselves with tear-gas, dogs, and guns in the vast areas where blacks live. Every young recruit is needed: there are boycotts, strikes, stay-at-homes, refusals to pay rent, all of which bring blacks into the streets with stones and home-product petrol bombs and sometimes grenades and AK-47s that have somehow been smuggled past the troops on the borders.

But there are thousands of young white men outside the army who are proficient in handling firearms. Only temporarily out of the army: all these healthy males have done their initial period of military service, but they are called up for short periods wherever an emergency within the Emergency arises. No one has had time enough in civilian life to lose his touch, handling an automatic rifle, or needs practice to get his eye in on target. Under command, and sometimes out of panic, they have shot chanting black schoolchildren, black mourners dispersing from those children's funerals, black rioters fleeing, black men and women who happened to go out for a pint of milk or a packet of cigarettes and crossed the path of an army patrol in the streets. Pick them off. They're all black. There is no time—it is no time—to distinguish the bystanders from the revolutionaries.

A large party of these healthy young white men from a university in the capital city of the country has been invited on a holiday that will also serve a useful purpose. Not exactly a study vacation, although the students will be shown round the meteorological station and have its complex and sophisticated weather-satellite system explained. More like a spree, taking them abroad to an unusual and little-known destination. They are going to the island under orders to shoot the cats. They are game for it. Among them is the young fellow who could have lost a blue eye by means of a stone thrown by a black, but was merely grazed to ooze a little of his Teraloyna blood-line. He is going, soon, to see through the oval of the aircraft window (pushing and shoving among his pals)—Look! Look down there—

The island we left for the mainland, all wrinkled and pleated in erosion, just topping out of the sea mists: the dark ravines where the goats held out long before felines did, the dark shores edged with bright surf, its movement frozen by the vertical distance of thousands of feet, before the aircraft slowly loses height.

He is going home to the island.

He is looking forward to the *jol* he and his mates will have, singing and stamping their army boots in the aircraft, the camp they will set up, the beer they will drink, and the prey they will pursue—this time grey, striped, ginger, piebald, tabby, black, white—all colours, abundant targets, doesn't matter which, kill, kill them all.

The Moment Before
the Gun Went Off

Marais Van der Vyver shot one of his farm labourers, dead. An accident, there are accidents with guns every day of the week—children playing a fatal game with a father's revolver in the cities where guns are domestic objects, nowadays, hunting mishaps like this one, in the country—but these won't be reported all over the world. Van der Vyver knows his will be. He knows that the story of the Afrikaner farmer—regional Party leader and Commandant of the local security commando—shooting a black man who worked for him will fit exactly *their* version of South Africa, it's made for them. They'll be able to use it in their boycott and divestment campaigns, it'll be another piece of evidence in their truth about the country. The papers at home will quote the story as it has appeared in the overseas press, and in the back-and-forth he and the black man will become those crudely-drawn figures on anti-apartheid banners, units in statistics of white brutality against the blacks quoted at the United Nations—he, whom they will gleefully be able to call 'a leading member' of the ruling Party.

People in the farming community understand how he must feel. Bad enough to have killed a man, without helping the Party's, the government's, the country's enemies, as well. They see the truth of that. They know, reading the Sunday papers, that when Van der Vyver is quoted saying he is 'terribly shocked', he will 'look after the wife and children', none of those Americans and English, and none of those people at home who want to destroy the white man's power will believe him. And how they will sneer when he even says of the farm boy (according to one paper, if you can trust any of those reporters), 'He was my friend, I always took him hunting with me.' Those city and overseas people don't know it's true: farmers usually have one particular black boy they like to take along with them in the lands; you could call it a kind of friend, yes, friends are not only your own white people, like yourself, you take into your house, pray with in church and work with on the Party committee. But how can those others know that? They don't want to know it. They think all blacks are like the big-mouth agitators in town. And Van der Vyver's face, in the photographs, strangely opened by distress—everyone in the district remembers Marais Van der Vyver as a little boy who would go away and hide himself if he caught you smiling at him, and everyone knows him now as a man who hides any change of expression round his mouth behind a thick, soft moustache, and in his eyes by always looking at some object in hand, leaf of a crop fingered, pen or stone picked up, while concentrating on what he is saying, or while listening to you. It just goes to show what shock can do; when you look at the newspaper photographs you feel like apologizing, as if you had stared in on some room where you should not be.

There will be an inquiry; there had better be, to stop the assumption of yet another case of brutality against farm workers, although there's nothing in doubt—an accident, and all the facts fully admitted by Van der Vyver. He made a statement when he arrived at the police station with the dead man in his bakkie. Captain Beetge knows him well, of course; he gave him brandy. He was shaking, this big, calm, clever son of Willem Van der Vyver, who inherited the old man's best farm. The black was stone dead, nothing to be done for him. Beetge will not tell anyone that after the brandy Van der Vyver wept. He sobbed, snot running onto his hands, like a dirty kid. The Captain was ashamed, for him, and walked out to give him a chance to recover himself.

Marais Van der Vyver left his house at three in the afternoon to cull a buck from the family of kudu he protects in the bush areas of his farm. He is interested in wildlife and sees it as the farmers' sacred duty to raise game as well as cattle. As usual, he called at his shed workshop to pick up Lucas, a twenty-year-old farmhand who had shown mechanical aptitude and whom Van der Vyver himself had taught to maintain tractors and other farm machinery. He hooted, and Lucas followed the familiar routine, jumping onto the back of the truck. He liked to travel standing up there, spotting game before his employer did. He would lean forward, braced against the cab below him.

Van der Vyver had a rifle and .300 ammunition beside him in the cab. The rifle was one of his father's, because his own was at the gunsmith's in town. Since his father died (Beetge's sergeant wrote 'passed on') no one had used the rifle and so when he took it from a cupboard he was sure it was not loaded. His father had never allowed a loaded gun in the house; he himself had been taught since childhood never to ride with a loaded weapon in a vehicle. But this gun was loaded. On a dirt track, Lucas thumped his fist on the cab roof three times to signal: look left. Having seen the white-ripple-marked flank of a kudu, and its fine horns raking through disguising bush, Van der Vyver drove rather fast over a pot-hole. The jolt fired the rifle. Upright, it was pointing straight through the cab roof at the head of Lucas. The bullet pierced the roof and entered Lucas's brain by way of his throat.

That is the statement of what happened. Although a man of such standing in the district, Van der Vyver had to go through the ritual of swearing that it was the truth. It has gone on record, and will be there in the archive of the local police station as long as Van der Vyver lives, and beyond that, through the lives of his children, Magnus, Helena and Karel—unless things in the country get worse, the example of black mobs in the towns spreads to the rural areas and the place is burned down as many urban police stations have been. Because nothing the government can do will appease the agitators and the whites who encourage them. Nothing satisfies them, in the cities: blacks can sit and drink in white hotels, now, the Immorality Act has gone, blacks can sleep with whites . . . It's not even a crime any more.

Van der Vyver has a high barbed security fence round his farmhouse and garden which his wife, Alida, thinks spoils completely the effect of her artificial stream with its tree-ferns beneath the jacarandas. There is an aerial soaring like a flag-pole in the back yard. All his vehicles, including the truck in which the black man died, have aerials that swing their whips when the driver hits a pot-hole: they are part of the security system the farmers in the district maintain, each farm in touch with every other by radio, twenty-four hours out of twenty-four. It has already happened that infiltrators from over the border have mined remote farm roads, killing white farmers and their families out on their own property for a Sunday picnic. The pot-hole could have set off a land-mine, and Van der Vyver might have died with his farm boy. When neighbours use the communications system to call up and say they are sorry about 'that business' with one of Van der Vyver's boys, there goes unsaid: it could have been worse.

It is obvious from the quality and fittings of the coffin that the farmer has provided money for the funeral. And an elaborate funeral means a great deal to blacks; look how they will deprive themselves of the little they have, in their lifetime, keeping up payments to a burial society so they won't go in boxwood to an unmarked grave. The young wife is pregnant (of course) and another little one, wearing red shoes several sizes too large, leans under her jutting belly. He is too young to understand what has happened, what he is witnessing that day, but neither whines nor plays about; he is solemn without knowing why. Blacks expose small children to everything, they don't protect them from the sight of fear and pain the way whites do theirs. It is the young wife who rolls her head and cries like a child, sobbing on the breast of this relative and that.

All present work for Van der Vyver or are the families of those who work; and in the weeding and harvest seasons, the women and children work for him, too, carried—

wrapped in their blankets, on a truck, singing—at sunrise
to the fields. The dead man's mother is a woman who can't
be more than in her late thirties (they start bearing children
at puberty) but she is heavily mature in a black dress between her own parents, who were already working for old
Van der Vyver when Marais, like their daughter, was a child.
The parents hold her as if she were a prisoner or a crazy
woman to be restrained. But she says nothing, does nothing.
She does not look up; she does not look at Van der Vyver,
whose gun went off in the truck, she stares at the grave.
Nothing will make her look up; there need be no fear that
she will look up; at him. His wife, Alida, is beside him. To
show the proper respect, as for any white funeral, she is
wearing the navy-blue-and-cream hat she wears to church
this summer. She is always supportive, although he doesn't
seem to notice it; this coldness and reserve—his mother
says he didn't mix well as a child—she accepts for herself
but regrets that it has prevented him from being nominated,
as he should be, to stand as the Party's parliamentary can-
didate for the district. He does not let her clothing, or that
of anyone else gathered closely, make contact with him.
He, too, stares at the grave. The dead man's mother and
he stare at the grave in communication like that between
the black man outside and the white man inside the cab
the moment before the gun went off.

The moment before the gun went off was a moment of
high excitement shared through the roof of the cab, as the
bullet was to pass, between the young black man outside
and the white farmer inside the vehicle. There were such
moments, without explanation, between them, although

often around the farm the farmer would pass the young man without returning a greeting, as if he did not recognize him. When the bullet went off what Van der Vyver saw was the kudu stumble in fright at the report and gallop away. Then he heard the thud behind him, and past the window saw the young man fall out of the vehicle. He was sure he had leapt up and toppled—in fright, like the buck. The farmer was almost laughing with relief, ready to tease, as he opened his door, it did not seem possible that a bullet passing through the roof could have done harm.

The young man did not laugh with him at his own fright. The farmer carried him in his arms, to the truck. He was sure, sure he could not be dead. But the young black man's blood was all over the farmer's clothes, soaking against his flesh as he drove.

How will they ever know, when they file newspaper clippings, evidence, proof, when they look at the photographs and see his face—guilty! guilty! they are right!—how will they know, when the police stations burn with all the evidence of what has happened now, and what the law made a crime in the past. How could they know that *they do not know*. Anything. The young black callously shot through the negligence of the white man was not the farmer's boy; he was his son.

Home

Lighted windows: cutouts of home in the night. When he came from his meeting he turned the key but the door was quickly opened from the inside—she was there, Teresa, a terribly vivid face. Her thin bare feet clutched the floorboards, she was in her cotton nightgown that in bed he would draw away tenderly, the curtain of her body.

—They've taken my mother. Robbie and Francie and my mother.—

He must have said something—No! Good God!—but was at once in awe of her, of what had happened to her while he was not there. The questions were a tumble of rock upon them: When? Where? Who told her?

—Jimmy just phoned from a call box. He didn't have enough change, we were cut off, I nearly went crazy, I didn't know what number to call back. Then he phoned again. They came to the house and took my mother and Francie as well as Robbie.—

—Your mother! I can't believe it! How could they take

that old woman? She doesn't even know what politics is—
what could they possibly detain her for?—

His wife stood there in the entrance, barring his and her
way into their home. —I don't know...she's the mother.
Robbie and Francie were with her in the house.—

—Well, Francie still lives with her, doesn't she. But why
was Robert there?—

—Who knows. Maybe he just went home.—

In the night, in trouble, the kitchen seems the room to
go to; the bedroom is too happy and intimate a place and
the living-room with its books and big shared desk and
pictures and the flowers he buys for her every week from
the same Indian street vendor is too evident of the life the
couple have made for themselves, apart.

He puts on the kettle for herb tea. She can't sit, although
he does, to encourage her. She keeps pulling at the lobes
of her ears in travesty of the endearing gesture with which
she will feel for the safety of the ear-rings he has given her.
—They came at four o'clock yesterday morning.—

—And you only get told tonight?—

—Nils, how was Jimmy to know? It was only when the
neighbours found someone who knew where he works that
he got a message. He's been running around all day trying
to find where they're being held. And every time he goes
near a police station he's afraid they'll take him in, as well.
That brother of mine isn't exactly the bravest man you could
meet...—

—Poor devil. D'you blame him. If they can take your
mother—then anybody in the family—

Her nose and those earlobes go red as if with anger, but
it is her way of fiercely weeping. She strokes harder and
harder the narrow-brained head of the Afghan hound, her

Dudu. She had never been allowed a dog in her mother's house; her mother said they were unclean. —It's so cold in that town in winter. What will my mother have to sleep on tonight in a cell.—

He gets up to take her to his arms; the kettle screams and screams, as if for her.

In bed in the dark, Teresa talked, cried, secure in the Afghan's warmth along one side of her, and her lover-husband's on the other. She did not have to tell him she cried because she was warm and her mother cold. She could not sleep—they could not sleep—because her mother, who had stifled her with thick clothing, suffocating servility, smothering religion, was cold. One of the reasons why she loved him—not the reason why she married him—was to rid herself of her mother. To love him, someone from the other side of the world, a world unknown to her mother, was to embrace snow and ice, unknown to her mother. He freed her of the family, fetid sun.

For him, she was the being who melted the hard cold edges of existence, the long black nights that blotted out half the days of childhood, the sheer of ice whose austerity was repeated, by some mimesis of environment, in the cut of his jaw. She came to him out of the houseful, streetful, of people as crowded together as the blood of different races mixed in their arteries. He came to her out of the silent rooms of an only child, with an engraving of Linnaeus, his countryman, in lamplight; and out of the scientist's solitary journeys in a glass bell among fish on the sea-bed—he himself had grown up to be an ichthyologist not a botanist. They had the desire for each other of a couple who would always be strangers. They had the special closeness of a couple who belonged to nobody else.

And that night she relived, relating to him, the meekness of her mother, the subservience to an unfeeling, angry man (the father, now dead), the acceptance of the ghetto place the law allotted to the mother and her children, the attempts even to genteel it with lace curtains and sprayed room-fresheners—all that had disgusted Teresa and now filled her with anguish because—How will a woman like my mother stand up to prison? What will they be able to do to her?—

He knew she was struggling with the awful discovery that she loved her mother, who was despicable; being imprisoned surely didn't alter the fact that her mother was so, proven over many omissions and years? He knew his Teresa well enough not to tell her the discovery was not shameful—that would bring it out into the open and she would accuse herself of sentimentality. Her *mother* was sentimental: those bronzed baby shoes of the men and women who had not grown up to be careful not to get into trouble, who had married a blond foreigner with a strange accent or taken to drink and bankruptcy, or got mixed up in politics, secret police files, arrests in the small hours of the morning. He listened and stroked her hair, sheltered her folded hand between his neck and shoulder as she cried and raged, pitying, blaming; and cursing—she who kept of her mother's genteelism at least her pure mouth—those fucking bastards of government and police for what they had done, done not only at four in the morning in that house with its smell of cooking oil and mothballs, but for generations, tearing up lives with their decrees on bits of paper, breaking down doors in power of arrest, shutting people off from life, in cells.

Later in the night when he thought she might at last have fallen asleep, she sat up straight: —What will she say? What does she know?—

She meant, about Robbie. Teresa and the brother, Robbie, were the ones who had got mixed up in politics. Teresa and her Swedish husband, living in this backwater coastal town in the company of marine biologists who were content to believe all species are interesting, and enquire no further into questions of equality, belonged to progressive organizations which walked the limit of but did not transgress legality, going no further than protest meetings. This was a respectable cover for the occasional clandestine support they gave Robbie, who really was mixed up, not just in avowals, but in the deeds of revolution. Sometimes it was money; sometimes it was an unannounced arrival in the middle of the night, with the need to go Underground for a day or two.

—Robbie won't have told her anything. You know how, even if he ever wanted to, she'd stop her ears.—

—It's not what she *knows*. She's never known anything about us. But they won't believe that! They'll go on interrogating her—

—Don't you think they'll soon discover it—that she's never known anything that would matter to them?—

His slow voice was the anchor from which she bobbed frantically. Suddenly her anger spilled in another direction. —What the hell got into him? What did Robbie go there for? How could he *dare* go to that house? How could he possibly not know that there, of all places, would be where they'd pick him up! The idiocy! The self-indulgence! What did he want, *a home-cooked meal*? I don't know what's gone wrong with the Movement, how they can let people behave so undisciplinedly, so childishly...How can we ever hope to see the end, if that's how they behave...The idiot! Handed over—*yes do come in and meet my mother and sister*—quite a social occasion in the family, all ready to be carted off to prison together. I hope he realizes what he's done. Some revolution, left to people like him... how *could* he go *near* that house—

They did not call each other by the endearments used commercially by every patronizing saleswoman and every affected actress—'love' and 'darling'—but had their own, in his language. —*Min lille loppa*, we don't know what his reasons might have been—

His 'little flea' beat the pillows with her fist, frightening her dog off the bed. —*There can't be any reason.* Except she ruined them all, for everything, for the revolution too— he's no different from the other brothers, in the end. He goes crawling back under mummy's skirt— You don't know those people, that family—

He went to the kitchen and brought her a glass of hot milk at four in the morning. While the milk was heating on the stove he stood at the kitchen window and put his palm on the pane, feeling the dark out there, the hour of the end of night into which, forty-eight hours before, mother, brother and sister had come, led to police cars.

In the morning, she didn't go to work. She was soiled and blurred by helplessness. He had been in that family house only a few awkward times over their seven years together, but he saw for the first time that she would resemble her mother if she were ever to grow old and afraid. With her lips drawn back in pain, her teeth looked long— the face of a victim. Distraught, her beauty dragged out of shape, there was the reversion to physical type that comes with age; some day he would become the listing old Scandinavian hulk who was his father or his uncle. He begged her to take one of his tranquillizers but she wouldn't—she had a horror of drugs, of drink, anything she had seen give others power over the individual personality; he had always privately thought this came subconsciously from her background, where people of one colour were submitted to the will of those of another.

He went to the Institute for an hour to set his team the tasks of the day and explain why both would be absent— she was employed there, too, in a humbler capacity, having had the opportunity, through their marriage and his encouragement, to satisfy her longing for some form of scientific education. When his colleagues asked what he was going to do he realized he didn't know. If it turned out that Teresa's family were detained under Section 29 they would have no access to lawyers or relatives. Between his colleagues' expressions of sympathy and support were (he saw) the regarding silences shared by them: they could have predicted this sort of disaster, inconceivable in their own lives, as a consequence of his kind of marriage.

He found her talking on the telephone. She was clutching the receiver in both hands, her feet were bare and wet, and the dog—the dog had undergone a change, too, shrunk to a bony frame plastered with fringes of wet fur.

She had bathed the dog? On this day?

She saw his face but was hysterically concentrated on what she was hearing; signalled, don't interrupt, be quiet! He put his arm round her and her one hand left the earpiece and groped up for his and held it tightly. She was cutting into the gabble on the other end: —But I must be able to reach you! Isn't there anywhere I can phone? If I don't hear from you, who will tell me what's happening?...Listen Jimmy, Jimmy, listen, I'm not blaming you...But if I can't phone you at work, then...No! No! That isn't good enough, d'you hear me, Jimmy—

There was a moment when he tried to hold steady the shifting gaze of her eyes. She put down the phone. —Call box. And I've forgotten the number he just gave me. I've been waiting the whole morning for him to call back, and now...I didn't know how to get myself away from sitting here looking at that phone...do anything, anything...He phoned just after you left and said he had a lawyer friend-of-a-friend, someone I've never heard of, he was going to find out details, something about approaching a magistrate—

The phone sprang alive again and she stared at it; he picked it up: there was the voice of her brother, hesitant, stumbling—Ma and them, they in under Section 29.—

She sat at the phone while he tried to activate the house as if it were a stopped clock. To keep them going there would have to be lunch (he cooked it), later the lights switched on, the time for news on television. But she couldn't eat not knowing if her mother was able to eat what there would be in a plate pushed through a cell door, she couldn't read by lamplight because there was darkness in a cell, and the news—there was no news when people were detained under Section 29. She telephoned friends and could not remember what they had said. She telephoned a doctor because she suddenly had the idea her mother had low blood pressure or high blood pressure—not sure which—and she wanted to know whether her mother could have a stroke and die, from the one, or collapse, from the other, in a prison? She did not want to go to bed. She brought out a small cracked photograph of her mother holding a baby (Robbie, she identified) with a cross-looking tiny girl standing by (herself). A piece of a man's coatsleeve showed where the rest of the photograph had been roughly cut off. The missing figure was her father. Exhausted, the two of them were up again until after midnight while she talked to him about her mother, was filled with curiosity and flashes of understanding about her mother, the monotony and smallness of her mother's life. —And it has to be this: the only big thing that's ever happened to her has to be this.— Her whole face trembled. He suffered with her. He was aware that it is a common occurrence that people talk with love about one they have despised and resented, once that person is dead. And to be in prison under Section 29, no one knows where, was to be dead to the world where one did not deserve to be loved.

In bed, she would not (of course) take a sleeping pill but they had each other. He made love to her while her tears smeared them both, and that put her blessedly to sleep. Now and then she gave the hiccuping sigh of a comforted child, and he woke at once and lifted his head, watching over her. There was a smell of clean dog-fur in the bed that third night.

Teresa.

He woke to find she was already bathed and dressed. She turned her head to him from the bedroom doorway when he spoke her name; her hair was drawn away tightly from her cheekbones and ears, held by combs. Again something had happened to her in his absence; this time while she was beside him, but they were parted in sleep. She was ready to leave the house long before it was time to go to work: going first to see an Indian woman lawyer whom they'd heard speak at protest meetings against detention without trial. He agreed it was a good idea. That was what must have come to her overnight, among these other things: if she was right about her mother's high tension (or whatever it was) Jimmy must contact the doctor who treated her and get a statement from him confirming a poor state of health—that might get her released or at least ensure special diet and treatment, inside. And something must be done about that house—it would be rifled in a week, in that neighbourhood. Somebody responsible must be found to go there and see that it was properly locked up—and tidy up, yes, the police would have turned everything upside down; if they arrest, they also search the scene of arrest.

—Shall I come with you?—

No, she had already phoned Fatima, she was waiting at her office. Teresa paused a moment, ready to go, rehearsing, he could see, what she had to say to the lawyer; blew him a kiss.

There were no more tears, no more tremblings. She came to the Institute straight from the lawyer's office, reported to him on the advice she had been given, put on her white coat and did her work. She found it hard to concentrate those first few days and had a dazed look about her, from the effort, when they met for lunch. They would seek a place to sit apart from others, in the canteen, like clandestine lovers. But it was not sweet intimacies their lowered voices exchanged. They were discussing what to do, what should be done, what could be done—and every now and then one or the other would look up to return the wave or greeting of a colleague, look up into the humid, cheerful room with the day's specials chalked on a board, people gathered round the coffee and tea and Coke dispensers, look out, through the expanse of glass the sea breathed on, to the red collage of flamboyants and jazzy poinsettias in the Institute's park—and her mother, brother and sister were in cells, somewhere. All the time. While they ate, while they worked, while they took the dog for his walk. For that progression of repetitions known as daily life went on; with only a realization of how strange it is, in its dogged persistence: what will stop it covering up what is really happening? In the cells; and here?

While he took care of that daily life (she had too much on her mind to be expected to shop and take clothes to the dry cleaner's) she spent all their spare time seeing lawyers, collecting and filling in applications to magistrates, chiefs of police, government officials, and consulting organizations concerned with the condition of detainees. She was no longer dazed; hair out of the way, her attention never deflected, determination hardened her gestures and emboldened her gentleness, sloughed it away. She importuned anyone she could use—that was how she put it—Maybe we can use So-and-so. He's supposed to be a good liberal, let's see what he'll do. Fatima says he's an old Stellenbosch buddy of the Commissioner of Police.— To ask for help apparently was too weak a demand, people would reply 'I'd help you if I could but...'; —We must pick people over whom there's public leverage of some sort.—

He marvelled at how she had come to this knowledge; she, who had always been so endearingly primly principled, even went to see a Nationalist ex-member of parliament who was said still to be close to the Minister of Justice. She, who had always been so sincere, revived acquaintance with people he and she had avoided as materialistic, incompatible, pushy, because now their connections might be of use. Her entire consciousness was a strategy. When she had managed—through Fatima's consultation with lawyers in the city where the mother, brother and sister were held— to get a parcel of blankets and clothing to them, she turned pressure on her mother's doctor, telephoning him at his home late at night to urge that the prison medical officer attend her mother; when that succeeded, she contacted the friend-of-a-friend, who lived in the city, to take food to the prison (dried fruit, yoghurt, these were the things, she ascertained from those who had been political prisoners, one most needed) and try and get the Chief Warder to accept it for her mother, Robbie and Francie. She was always on the telephone; he brought her plate to her from their interrupted meals, where she sat, elbows on knees, on a stool—it was her corner, now, just as Dudu had his particular place under the table. That terrible ivy, daily life. How to pull it away and see—what?

She was constantly on the telephone because what was happening in the cells was far away, in Johannesburg. She became stern with impatience—sympathy irritated her and he had to realize that, for all their closeness, apartness together, he couldn't really claim to be feeling what she was feeling. Every enquiry or instruction from her had to be referred through a third person. Jimmy's timidity made him even less intelligent, she said, than he had ever been. He wasn't to be relied on and he was the only member of the family *there*. Where she should be; every time some proxy bungled, it came up: she should be there. And then it was he who became distraught, couldn't concentrate on anything but the cold anxiety that she would go there, walk into the waiting car of the Security Police, he saw them ready for her, counting on her coming to that house, to that prison where her mother, brother and sister were held. Hadn't he said to her, of Jimmy's fears, that it was a fact that *anyone* in the family ...? And she was the one who had connections with Robbie beyond blood ties!

—*Exactly!* They might turn up *here* any time and take you and me. Both of us. How do we know what's come out, in there ... what he might have told my mother or poor frightened Francie—my sister's only nineteen, you know ...Those two women'll never stand up under interrogation from those beasts, they couldn't even judge what's compromising and what isn't.—

His physical size seemed to hamper him when opposing the will that tempered her slender body. He spoke, and it was as if he made some clumsy, inappropriate move towards her. —But they haven't. I mean, thank god they haven't. Maybe they don't know about you.—

She gave a disparaging half-grunt, half-laugh.

—Maybe no one's said anything about us ... you. But if you go there, at once they'll decide they might as well see what you know. And there is something to be got out of you, isn't there.—

She gestured away the times her brother had appeared for refuge; the packets of papers that had been hidden under research documents about the habits of fish, in the desk of the Institute's Swedish expert.

—Teresa, I won't let you go!— He had never before spoken to her in that voice, probably it was the ugly voice of her father—he felt he had struck her a blow; but it was on his own sternum that his fist had fallen. He was shouting.

—I will not have it! I'll go, if someone must, I'll go, I'm not one of the family!—

The dissension was like a sheet of newspaper that catches alight, swells and writhes with flame, and quickly dies to a handful of black membrane.

She dropped the idea. He thirsted with relief; she watched him go to the cupboard and pour himself a whisky, but she didn't need anything like that. Every few days, something would happen that would precipitate the ordeal all over again. By now she had made connections that had ways of smuggling news out of the prison: Robbie was on a hunger strike, her mother and Francie had been moved to another prison. Why? She ought to be there to find out. The lawyer's application to the Minister for her mother's and Francie's release was awaiting decision. She ought to be there to see if something couldn't be done to hasten it. Her husband brought in friends to back him up; he, they, wouldn't hear of her going.

She took leave of absence from the Institute. He didn't know whether *that* was a good idea or not. At least work was a distraction, thinking about other matters, talking to people who had other concerns. This one had been cleaned out—a burglary, lost everything—*things*? He saw the question in her face, flung back. That one had a dying wife—*death*? Of course, death's natural; he reflected that if her sixty-something-year-old mother had become ill and died, in that house, it would have been an event to accept.

So the practical preoccupations of her mother's and siblings' detention became her work, as well. Even her few pleasures—no, wrong word—her few small satisfactions were part of the disaster: there was the news that a banner calling for the release of her mother, brother and sister had been displayed at a meeting of a liberation movement broken up by police and dogs. There were messages from the movement in exile for which Robbie was active: they preferred this lawyer rather than that to be engaged on his behalf. And the fact that they knew to contact her drew her into another kind of cell, of new associates for whom detention was a hazard like a traffic fine, and clandestinity with all its cunning a code for survival in or out of prison.

It was on their advice that she started sleeping away from home. Well, it was a disinterested confirmation of the fears he had had for her; and, at the same time, of her conviction that she could just as well be picked up there as in the region of her mother's house or place of imprisonment. She went to this good friend or that. —I may be at Addie's tonight, if not with Stephen and Joanna.— She held him tightly a moment, buried Dudu's slim snout against her before she slipped out, and she would be back early in the morning for breakfast. But he lay in their bed full of deserted desire for her, although they had not made love for weeks, not since the second night after the news came. He sensed she was ashamed of their joy happening while the others—that family—were out of human touch in prison. Once, he gave in to the temptation to hear her voice and phoned her where she said she would sleep, but she wasn't there; and of course it would defeat the whole purpose of her absence if the friend who answered the call were to have told him where she had moved to; it was more than likely that the phone he was using at his bedside was tapped. He was too ashamed, next day, to confess to her his childish impulse.

She never wore her hair loose, now. No doubt it was because she didn't have the heart to spend time putting it up in rollers and brushing it out, innocently enjoying the sight of it in the mirror, as she used to. Yet she looked differently beautiful; a woman becomes another woman when she changes the way she wears her hair. The combs scragged it away from her cheekbones and eye-hollows. She looked like a dusky Greta Garbo (he was just old enough to remember Greta Garbo). When the front door banged and she came in to breakfast in the mornings he felt—and it was like a fear—that he was falling in love with her. But how unpleasant and ridiculous, he had loved her for seven years, Teresa, Teresa—there was no need for abandoning that, starting something new.

And then there came to him the mad thought—mad!—that it was not he who was falling in love with her; someone else was. There was the mark of it on her, in the different beauty. *She was the way someone else saw her.* That was what he confronted himself with when she arrived in the mornings.

There was a day when the hair was wet, twisted up and the combs pushed in any-old-how.

—The sea looked so cool, I couldn't resist a dip on the way.—

—I'm glad, *min lille loppa*, was it lovely?—

At the time he was tenderly pleased, as at the sign of recovery to a normal interest in life by an invalid. But walking through the Institute's aquarium, while the fish mouthed at him he was overcome by what could not be said: who was it who swam with her, and she must have been naked, or only in her panties, because surely she didn't take a swimsuit with her when she went away to elude the Security Police at night.

An hour or two later he could not believe he could have

thought so cheaply about her, Teresa, Teresa. There was a little beach where he and she had often swum in the nude, sheltered by rocks; it was their beach she would have been to, alone, without him.

Because he had these moments of thinking badly of her, he became shy of her. They had always shared the discomfort of one another's small indispositions—her period pains, his bouts of indigestion if he sat too long crouched over a microscope. Now he suffered, all to himself, an embarrassing ailment, a crawling sensation round the anus. It seemed to him it must be one of the signs of middle age, the beginning of the deterioration of the nervous system. What would such a distasteful detail mean to her, at this time? Getting older, decaying, was natural. And she was young: why should she want to be bothered with his backside while her mother and brother and sister were still in prison—it was nine weeks now. And she had a young lover.

Oh why did these thoughts come!

Why should she not have found a lover, young like herself, brought up in comradely poverty, someone who had already been in prison, whose métier, outwitting those bastards of policemen, warders, government officials, was newly her own?

And now, every sign could be interpreted that way. She, who had always been so love-hungry, passionate, had not come to him in weeks and had created an atmosphere round herself that made it indelicate for him to come to her. When she had slept out and arrived home early in the morning, she could have slipped into their bed, where he still lay; she didn't. The night he had phoned Stella's flat—she wasn't there; and how had Stella sounded? Hadn't the voice been constrained? Lying? Covering up? Teresa, Teresa. He was thinking about all this *in Swedish*. What did that mean? He was retreating, going back to what he was before they made their life apart from the past, together . . . she was thrusting him back there, leaving him, she had a lover. He began to try to find out who it was. When she talked about fellow members of the Detainees' Support Committee he listened for the recurrence of certain names; and there was new dismay for him—it might even be that she was having an affair with someone else's husband. Teresa! At the occasional parties they had gone to, over seven years, she had not even danced with any man because he did not dance; she would hold his hand and watch.

And then one night—no it was morning already, behind the curtains—the dog jumped off the bed and whined and he heard the front door latch click. He waited but she did not come into the bedroom; he must have fallen asleep again, waiting, and when he woke he felt the silence of an empty house. In the kitchen was a note: 'I'll be gone for a few days. Don't worry. *Lille loppa*.' It was the kind of note left, these days, by people like Robbie, people like the ones she mixed with. If they had to disappear; if they didn't want anyone who might be questioned about their whereabouts to get into trouble with the police: the less you know, the better for you. But he knew. He was sure, now. Perhaps it was even her way of letting him know. If the police came, he could tell them: She has gone away with a lover.

He could not imagine her without himself—just as she, when it all began, could not imagine whether her mother would be able to eat or sleep in prison. Teresa across the table from someone who would put dead flesh on her plate (theirs was a vegetarian home) and she would eat it. Teresa in one of the cotton nightgowns; if she could take a swimsuit in her handbag for a secret early morning rendezvous she would not hesitate to take the nightgown. Unlike Teresa, he drank whisky and swallowed sleeping pills so that he might not think any further. But he dreamt horribly, from the mixture. In the dream they had a child who was playing at the water's edge on their beach, where he was making love to Teresa, and he fiercely pursued his climax while he knew a high surf was washing the child out to sea. He woke like a schoolboy, wet with the dream.

Standing at his tanks in the Institute he followed the movements, currents and streamers, rose, violet, yellow and blue, of the tropical fish from these southern waters that would have devoured the drowned body of the child, and he thought of the scrubbed satiny floors, the white muslin curtains and the white-trunked birch trees of the house with the silent rooms he had inherited outside Stockholm. He had not thought he would ever have to live there again.

After three days, she telephoned the Institute just before noon.

—Where are you?—

—Here. Dudu's head's in my lap!— She was laughing.

He left at once, and again, as he put his key in the door it was opened from the inside. She held out her hands, palm up; he had to take them, and did so slowly. They went into the kitchen where he saw she had been eating bread and avocado, hungrily spreading crumbs, in her way. The dog was sniffing her over to sense where she had been and what she had done, and he, too, wanted and feared to get the scent of her betrayal.

She sat back in a kitchen chair and faced him.

—I've seen her. And I've got notes from Francie and Robbie, smuggled out. She's all right. I knew you'd stop me if I told you I was going.—

She lifted her shoulders, shook her head, smiling, closing the subject.

Perhaps there was no lover? He saw it was true that she had left him, but it was for them, that house, the dark family of which he was not a member, her country to which he did not belong.

A Journey

On my way back home from Europe I saw a beautiful woman with a very small baby and a son of about thirteen. They were sitting across the aisle from me in the aircraft. The baby could not have been more than ten days old. It had abundant black fine hair standing up from its head the way hair lifts from a scalp under water; as if the hair had been combed, floating, by the waters of the womb. The pathetic little bent legs had never been used. The eyelids were thick and lifted slowly, a muscular impulse still being tested, revealing an old and wondering gaze: eyes very dark, but no colour that could be described as black or blue. Perhaps colour has something to do with focus and it was focusing only now and then—that was the wondering—on the face of the mother. Or rather the *gaze* of the mother. She would look into its face, and its eyes would open like buds. The strange concentration between them was joined, frequently, by that of the boy.

The boy was beautiful as his mother. In words beauty

can be suggested only by its immediate signal. Theirs was of clarity. Their identical round brows were clear horizons, their nostrils and earlobes appeared translucent, their skin, lips and eyes had the colouring of portraits in stained glass. The baby was unlike either of them. It was the presence of someone absent; and yet it was so intensely theirs. She parted her clothes (fashionable, expensively, discreetly dressed, she was) and although I couldn't see her breast I could tell from the angle of the baby's head in the crook of her arm and the slight bobbing movement of its hairy head that it was sucking. The boy and the mother leant over it—this process—reverently. Once I saw her put her well-used but beautiful hand round the curve of the boy's head and hold it there a moment. A trinity.

From time to time the boy suddenly became the child he was; he was working at a puzzle or game supplied for youngsters along with the usual handout of head-sets and slippers. He was turned away, then; but kept being drawn back to that contemplation in which he served. Literally: he was up and down during the night, taking the baby's dirty napkins to be disposed of in the toilet, bringing plastic cups of water which his lips and his mother's touched indiscriminately. Then the baby slept in its portable cot on the floor and the two of them, the dividing arm between their seats removed, slept as a single form disposed under aircraft blankets. They had even covered the separate identity of their faces—no doubt against the cabin lights.

They left the plane when it landed to refuel in the middle of Africa. That airport recently had been closed for the period when there was an attempted coup in the country; distorted in the convex window of the plane I could see burned-out military vehicles, two of the letters that spelled as the airport's name across the façade of the terminal the name of the country's President were missing, and dogs were foraging at the margin of the runway.

She had the baby in her arms. The boy carried their bulky hand-luggage, hovering protectively close as she stepped through the door onto the gangway that had been rolled into place. My window was a lens with a more restricted range of vision than the human eye: mine could not follow them across the tarmac to the terminal building, I don't know if they hurried anticipatedly, excitedly to what was awaiting them there, I don't know where they had been, why they had gone, or what they were coming back to. I know only that the baby was so young it must have been born elsewhere, they were bringing it to this place for the first time, this was its first journey. I continued mine; they had disappeared. They exist only in the alternate lives I invent, the unknown of what happened to them preceding the journey, and the unknown of what was going to happen at its end.

I'm thirteen. I'd had my birthday when I went away with my mother to have the baby in Europe. There isn't a good hospital in the country where my father is posted—he's Economic Attaché—so we went back where my parents come from, the country he represents wherever we live. I know it only from holidays with my grandma because I was born when they were on another posting.

I'd been my parents' child—the only one—so long. I always wanted brothers and sisters but never had any. And then, round about my twelfth birthday I noticed it, something went wrong in our house—I mean the house we are living in on this posting. My mother and father were almost silent at meals. The private language we used to speak together—cat-language—we didn't use any more. You see, I'm allowed to have cats as pets but not dogs, because cats can almost fend for themselves when we get another posting and they have to be left behind; we have a different kind of voice for each of the three cats I have here, and we used to pretend the cats were making remarks about us. For instance, if I was eating with my elbows on the table, my father would use a cat voice to tell me I had bad manners, and if my father forgot to fill up my mother's wineglass my mother would use her special cat voice to complain she'd been left out. But the cats stopped speaking; they became just cats. I couldn't be the only one to use their voices. A child can't use even a cat voice to ask: what's the matter? You can't ask grown-ups that.

The three of us stopped going swimming together. We love swimming and before we used to go often to the Consul-General's pool. But my father made me learn to play squash with him and he took me on spear-fishing trips with men. The sea is very rough here, it's horrible being thrown about by breakers full of bits of plastic and rotten fruit from the harbour before the boat gets to the place where you dive. These were things my mother didn't do: play squash, spear-fish. I told her about the sea, but she didn't say anything to my father, she didn't take my part. It was a bit like what happened to me: as if she couldn't use a cat voice to tell him.

He—my father—would hug me, just suddenly, for no reason; not when he was going away anywhere, but just leaving the room, or if we met at the top of the stairs. And my mother encouraged me to spend the weekends with friends. To sleep away from them, my mother and father. I cried once, by myself, because she seemed to want me out of the house. It wasn't as if they could need to be alone together, to talk without a kid around the way grown-ups sometimes do even though they love you; they would sit there at meals with nothing to talk to each other about, just quiet. The cats would get scraps and say nothing.

And yet it was that time that it happened—the baby. They made the baby. My mother told me one day: I'm going to have a baby. She looked at me very anxiously. To see if I'd mind. I didn't mind. I know about sex, of course, how she'd got pregnant, what my father had done with her, although they didn't smile at each other, didn't tease or laugh at each other any more. Nine months is a long time. I turned thirteen. My father was away a lot, round the country. Once she used to go with him, leaving me for a day or two, but now she didn't go because of the baby growing, she said. So we were alone together. We watched her changing, the baby changing her. I know some boys aren't allowed to see their mother's breasts but she used to swim topless like the other ladies at the Consul-General's, and I was used to seeing how pretty hers were, not the hard-looking little kind that stick out on girls a few years older than I am, but not the hanging kind that swing when the woman gets up, either—soft and quite far apart, because my mother has broad shoulders. Now the breasts filled up, I felt them against me like plastic bags filled with water when she put her arms round me to kiss me good night, and I saw above the low neck of her nightdress that they were changing, becoming pink and mottled. It was strange, I thought of a chameleon slowly blotching from one colour to another when you put it on a flower. But it was the baby that was doing it. When it began to move inside her she put my hand on her stomach, for me to feel. More like hearing than feeling; it knocked very softly. So I put my ear there. My mother put her hand on my head and I listened and felt. A bit like Morse code, I told her: it would give three or four quick taps and then stop, and start again. What was it saying, doing, in there? We'd laugh, and make up things, like we used to do with the cats. But it was only the two of us and the baby; He wasn't there.

Sometimes, those months, in a dream I would feel against me the breasts that were changing for the baby and the dream would become one of those it's normal for boys to have (my mother and father explained before I began to have them). There's nothing to be ashamed of, you should enjoy those dreams; I just put my pyjamas in the wash. Another time I dreamt I put my ear to where the baby was and suddenly the big hard stomach turned into a goldfish bowl, and the baby was swimming around in there and I was watching it. A golden baby, a big golden fish like the ones He went after, under the sea. But this one was ours— my mother and me—in her bowl, and in the dream I was taking care of it.

I was the first to see the baby. I saw it when it was exactly 40 minutes old. I was the first to see my mother with the baby. I was in the hospital waiting-room with my grandmother and when the nurse said we could come and look I ran ahead and I was there before anyone—nurses don't count, it's not theirs. My mother asked the time and when I told her she said the baby was exactly 40 minutes old, she had promised me she would remember to ask the doctor the time the very moment it was born, and she had kept her promise. We looked at the baby together, its ears, its feet and hands; everything was all right. Its eyes didn't open. We were surprised by its hair; it had a lot of wet-looking black hair that stood up on its head as she carefully dried it with the edge of a blanket. We have pale brown hair; my grandmother says my mother was born bald, and my mother says I was, too. The baby was not like us at all. Neither of us said who it was like. The baby was only what we couldn't have imagined, what had been tapping messages and changing her body all that time, and had suddenly come out. For the next week we watched it changing itself, beginning to live outside my mother, live with my mother and me.

It was born so healthy the doctor said we could fly back with it when it was only nine days and sixty-two minutes old (I made that calculation while we were waiting for our flight to be called). They gave us the bulkhead seats and there was plenty of room for the baby's stuff—the seat across the aisle was vacant, only a lady with grey hair in the other window seat. We didn't speak to her. We didn't have to talk to anyone, it was just us alone. I arranged our big canvas bag so my mother could rest her feet up on it. Then I fitted in the baby's cot and there was still room for my legs, although my legs are getting long, my mother's had to pick out the hems of my jeans. The baby was very good. It only cried when it wanted to feed, and then softly, you could hardly hear it above the sound of the air rushing through the jet engines and people talking in the rows behind us. It was more as if it was talking to us, my mother and me, than actually crying. I lifted it out of the cot each time so's my mother wouldn't have to bend and put her feet down. It sucked away just as if it was on the ground and not up at an altitude of 30,000 feet travelling at 500 miles an hour.

Its eyes were able to open by then. They are big and dark and shiny. It looked at us, it distinctly looked from my mother to me while we watched it feed—my mother said it was wondering where it had seen us before and forgotten us. That's how it seemed to her. I thought it was curious about us. We both kissed its head often. That funny hair it has.

The steward gave me an acrostic game but I'm used to my computer games and I didn't find it too interesting. I tried it while my mother had her eyes shut, resting (it's tiring, feeding a baby from your own body), but that meant I might miss something the baby was doing—yawning, pulling faces—so I didn't keep on long. I like old-fashioned rock-'n'-roll my mother remembers she used to dance to and I found the dial number to turn to for it, but I took off the head-set every few minutes because I thought I heard my mother speaking to me. She might need something; feeding a baby dehydrates you, I had to fetch those plastic cups of water from the dispenser for her, and I took the baby's napkins, in the plastic bags we'd specially brought along, to dump in the lavatory. I pushed them through the flap marked 'Airsickness Containers'. We had prepared everything for the journey, we didn't need to ask anyone for a single thing. We made ourselves comfortable and slept, the baby quite safe. We knew even with our eyes closed and the blankets over our heads (my mother is sensitive to light and the eyeshade she was given was too thin) that the baby was there.

Suddenly my mother was saying to me, Here's the river. I woke up and it was light and I leant over her and the baby and saw far down through the window the whole river, whose other bank you can't see from the side where we're posted—it's such a wide river. We were there. I didn't think about Him waiting for us. I had so much to do: packing the baby's stuff away, getting our coats from the overhead bin, making sure for my mother we wouldn't forget anything. Remember, we'd never arrived with the baby before, it was the first time ever. The baby did not know that posting it had lived in, beginning when something went wrong, growing inside my mother all those months when He was away most of the time. I felt very excited, landing with something new, new. I felt new. I came down the gangway behind my mother who had the baby in front of her, in her arms the way I'd seen her carry an armful of flowers. I carried everything else of ours—the canvas bag, the coats, the cot. We came quickly through immigration because people let you go first in the queue when you have a baby. But we had to wait for the luggage. Before the conveyer belt had even started moving, the baby began to cry, it had woken up and was hungry again. The luggage was a long time coming and the baby didn't stop. My mother sat down on our canvas bag and I knelt in front of her so people wouldn't see when she opened her clothes and fed the baby. It was very greedy, all of a sudden, and it grabbed her and pulled—like a little goat, my mother said, and we were smiling at it, saying to each other, just see that, it's going to choke, it's gorging, listen to it gulp, when I looked up and saw Him where they had allowed him in through Customs. They always let him in where others can't go, because He's the Economic Attaché. I saw Him finding us, seeing us for the first time, watching my mother and me feeding the baby, He might even have been able to see her breast from where he was, He's tall. He threw up his head and his mouth opened, He was happy, He was coming to get us. Then I felt full of joy and strength, it was like being angry, but much better, much much better. I saw him looking at us and he knew that I saw him, but I didn't look back at him.

The silence is over.

That is what has been repeating in his head since the alarm clock woke him with its electronic peeps at five this morning. He phoned the airport before he got out of bed, and while hearing the stretched Glockenspiel tape they entertain you with when you're waiting for Information to answer, that phrase was counterpointing again and again, himself speaking inside himself: 'The silence is over'. Because the love affair is over. The silence in which the love affair was hidden, precious and thrilling, something she must not be allowed to touch with a word, now seems an agony endured. More than a year of confidences, feelings unexpressed, emotions, anecdotes lie painfully trapped, layer on layer, constricted within him. But she has given birth; he wonders how it will be to see her again, rid of her burden. Her body as it was before, when he used to see it: he saw her only clothed while her body was growing, filling, she stopped undressing in front of him because they could not speak.

The flight is expected in on time. He puts on linen trousers and sandals, the air-conditioner continues to stutter and shudder and soon, thank God, he won't notice it any more because it won't be the only noise in an empty house. He shaves but puts the cologne back on the shelf because—like an impulse of nausea the morning after a night out, this comes—it is what he used to smell of when he came home from the bed and scent of another woman, an unsuccessful disguise, he knows, because it was obvious he had showered after love-making, you don't come from the Consulate offices with wet hair. The madness of it! Just as during that year he couldn't think about his wife, didn't see her even when she was sitting across the table from him, so now he is too preoccupied to visualize the woman he couldn't keep away from even for a day. Driving on the airport road over fallen yellow flowers of cassia trees he feels memory like a hand alternately scalded and balmed—fear of the terrible experience of the wonderful love affair that belongs to this place, this posting, as the trees do, and gratitude to the endurance of these trees, this posting where he is about to be restored. There were tanks rolling along this road not long ago, and it's unevenly patched with fresh tarmac where it was blown up. But the familiar trees full of yellow blossom are still here. So is he.

He parks the car innocently, now, right out in the open; it has not brought him to any clandestine destination where he would arrive already with an erection. He walks slowly into the airport building because this passage between low hedges of Christ's-thorn and hibiscus propped up like standard roses—nobody would believe what survives an attempted coup, while people are shot—is the way towards something that is both old and new—nobody would believe what a man and woman can survive, between themselves.

This decaying airport he has been in and out of impatiently many times is going to be where it happens; how strange that is. How appropriately inappropriate definitive places are. He is early, at first the arrival hall is empty, bins overflowing with beer cans seem blown away against the walls, the worn red rubber flooring glittering under its spills and dirt stretches vast, he is alone in the perspective of a de Chirico painting...

These wisps of philosophical generalizing, fragments of the culture and education which overlay the emotions that drive life, drift irrelevantly away from him. She is coming home with a live baby. That flesh, that fact is what has resulted of one night when he returned from a weekend trip with that woman and was so angry at his wife's forlornness, her need of comfort he couldn't give, for something he couldn't say, that he made love to her. Fucked her. It was not even good fucking because he had been making love to the other woman, rapturously, tenderly, hardly sleeping for two nights. It was an act shameful to them both, his wife and himself. It did not serve as a way of speaking to one another. More like a murder than a conception. If it hadn't been for that horrible night there would have been no baby and—a clutch of fear at the danger so narrowly escaped—he wouldn't be waiting here now, the love affair might have ploughed on through his life leaving nothing standing.

The gatherings of people who hang about these airports all day rather than arrive or depart are beginning to humanize and domesticate the surreal vacuum of the hall. The men come in talking, there seems always, day or night, something for black men to explain, argue, exclaim over to one another. They are surely never lonely. The turbaned women are clusters rather than individuals, children clinging to and climbing about the mothers' robes, whose symbols of fish and fruit and the face of the President circled with a message of congratulation on his sixtieth birthday are their picture books. The blacks take their children everywhere, they sleep under their mothers' market stalls, they

nod, tied on their mothers' backs, through the beer halls—
these people never part from their children, at least while
they are pre-adolescent. After that, in this country, the boys
may be abducted by the rebel army or drafted beardless
into the President's youth labour corps; often not seen at
home again, after all that closeness when they're little, all
that flesh-contact of warmth and skin-odours that is—love?
He tried to keep the boy out of the silence, to speak to him.
To show love. That is, to do things with him. But the fact
is the boy is not manly, he's not adventurous—he's too
beautiful. Too much like her, her delicate skin round the
eyes, her nacreous ears, her lips the way they are when she
wakes in the morning, needing no paint. Lovely in a
woman—yes, *lover*ly, what a man wants, desirable and wel-
coming (how could he ever have forgotten that, even for
one year in fifteen?). But not in a boy. The boy can swim
like a fish but he sulked when he was taken spear-fishing
with adults, with his father; an expedition any other boy
would have been proud to be included in. And those times
when *love* suddenly, for a moment, didn't mean the other
woman, when it was a rush of longing for flesh-contact and
the skin-odours of one's own child, to have that child
cling—he didn't understand, he only submitted. As his
mother did, that one night.

He doesn't allow himself to look at his watch. There is
still at least a quarter of an hour to go. That night—that
she should have conceived that night. When the boy was
younger they had tried for another child. Nothing happened. All the time when it would have been conceived out
of joy, when they still desired each other so much and so
often! And of course that's the main reason why the boy
has been spoilt—as he thinks of it, he doesn't mean only

in the sense of over-indulged as an only child. And it is also *his* fault—part of that madness! No point in sorrowing over it now (a spasm of anguish) but when she conceived out of the willed lust of anger and shame he felt at the sight of his victim, he didn't want to see what was happening to her, he didn't want to see her belly growing and she didn't want him to see her. She was alone days and nights on end with the boy, poor little devil. And even when the time came, only last month, for the baby to be born, he sent the boy with her to Europe for the birth. He sent her away with an immature thirteen-year-old as her only companion when his own place was with her (there is a hoarse twanging murmur over the public address system but he makes out it is the departure announcement for another plane) *his own place was with her*: the throbbing of the words starts up again immediately his attention is turned from the distraction.

This onslaught of the past year rising from the places in himself where it was thrust away both denies his actual presence here in the airport hall where people beside him are eating cold cassava porridge and drinking Coke from the refreshment and curio shop that has just removed its shutters, and at the same time makes momentous every detail of this place, this scene. For the rest of his life, he knows, he will be able to feel the split in the seat beneath him where the stuffing spills like guts. He will be able to arrange the graduated line of ebony elephants from charm-bracelet to door-stop size, the malachite beads, copper bangles, and model space monsters imprisoned in plastic bubbles against card among the dead cockroaches in the shop's window that he walks past and past again. These are his witnesses. The tawdry, humble and banal bear testimony to the truth; the splendid emotions of a love affair are the luxurious furnishings of the lie.

A green star on the Arrivals and Departures indicator is flashing. He stands up from the broken seat. It doesn't matter that the announcement comes as a burble, he catches the number of the flight, the green star keeps flashing. The unhappy night when he forced himself to make love to his wife and she conceived this baby he's awaiting— that's all over. He is her husband again, her lover. He has come back to her in a way she will realize the moment she steps off the plane and he embraces her. The end of a journey he took, away from her, and the end of her journey, now, will meet and they'll be whole again. With the baby. The baby is the wholeness she is carrying off the plane to him and he'll receive.

The ordinary procedure of privilege is taking place: the Customs man recognizes him as usual, someone attached to a foreign consulate, someone who doesn't have to abide by the rules for local people with their bundles and relatives. Right through, sir, thank you sir. He has passed a checkpoint this way countless times; but this time replicates no time.

There they are.

Through a glass screen he sees them near the baggage conveyer belt. There they are. A little apart from the other passengers ringed round the belt. What's the matter with the boy? Why doesn't that boy stand by ready to lift off the baggage?

They are apart from the rest of the people, she is sitting on that huge overnight bag, he sees the angle of her knees, sideways, under the fall of a wide blue skirt. And the boy is kneeling in front of her, actually kneeling. His head is bent and her head is bent, they are gazing at something. Someone. On her lap, in the encircling curve of her bare arm. The baby. The baby's at her breast. The baby's there; its reality flashes over him in a suffusion of blood. He pauses, to hold the moment. He doesn't know how to deal with it. And in that moment the boy turns his face, his too beautiful face, and their gaze links.

Standing there, he throws his head back and gasps or laughs, and then pauses again before he will rush towards them, his wife, the baby, claim them. His cry flings a noose towards the boy. Catch! Catch! But the boy is looking at him with the face of a man, and turns back to the woman as if she is his woman, and the baby his begetting.

Spoils

In the warmth of the bed your own fart brings to your nostrils the smell of rotting flesh: the lamb chops you devoured last night. Seasoned with rosemary and with an undertaker's paper frill on the severed rib-bones. Another corpse digested.

'Become a vegetarian, then.' She's heard it all too many times before; sick of it, sick of my being sick of it. Sick of the things I say, that surface now and then.

'I want no part of it.'

We are listening to the news.

'What? What are you going on about. *What?*'

What indeed. No: which. Which is it I choose to be no part of, the boy who threw a stone at the police, had both his arms broken by them, was sodomized by prisoners into whose cell he was thrown, the kidnapped diplomat and the group (men, as I am a man, women, as she is a woman) who sent his fourth finger by mail to his family, the girl doused with petrol and burned alive as a traitor, those starved by drought or those drowned by flood, far away, the nineteen-year-old son of Mr and Mrs killed by the tremendous elemental thrill of 220 volts while using an electric spray gun on his motorbike, near by. The planned, devised, executed by people like myself, or the haphazard, the indifferent, executed senselessly by elemental forces. *Senselessly*. Why is there more sense in the conscious acts that make corpses? Consciousness is self-deception. Intelligence is a liar.

'You're not having great thoughts. That's life.'

Her beauty-salon philosophy. Stale, animal, passive. Whether I choose or not; can't choose, can't want *no part*.

The daily necrophilia.

'Become a vegetarian, then!'

Among other people no one would ever think there was anything wrong. He is aware of that; she is aware of his being aware, taking some kind of pride in appearing exactly as they have him in their minds, contributing to their gathering exactly what his place in it expects of him. The weekend party invited to a lodge on a private game reserve will include the practical, improvising man, the clown who burns his fingers at the camp fire and gets a laugh out of it, the woman who spends her time preparing to feed everyone, the pretty girl who perks up the company sexually, the good-timer who keeps everyone drinking until late, the quiet one who sits apart contemplating the bush, one or two newcomers, for ballast, who may or may not provide a measure of serious conversation. Why not accept? No? *Well*.

What else has he in mind that will please him better? Just say.

Nothing.

There you are!

He, in contrast to the clown, is the charmer, the wit. He knows almost everyone's foibles, he sets the anecdotes flowing, he provides the gentle jibes that make people feel themselves to be characters.

Whatever their temperaments, all are nature lovers. That is nothing to be ashamed of—surely, even for him. Their love of the wild brings them together—the wealthy couple who own the reserve and lodge rather than racehorses or a yacht, the pretty girl who models or works in public relations, the good-timer director of a mining house, the adventurous stockbroker, the young doctor who works for a clerk's salary in a hospital for blacks, the clowning antique dealer ... And he has no right to feel himself superior—in seriousness, morality (he knows that)—in this company, for it includes a young man who has been in political detention. That one is not censorious of the playground indulgences of his fellow whites, so long as the regime he has risked his freedom to destroy, will kill to destroy, lasts. That's life.

Behaving—undetectably—as what is expected of one is also a protection against fear of what one really is, now. Perhaps what is seen to be, is himself, the witty charmer. How can he know? He does it so well. His wife sees him barefoot, his arms round his knees on the viewing deck from which the company watches buffalo trampling the reeds down at the river, hears the amusing asides he makes while gazing through field-glasses, notices the way he has left his shirt unbuttoned in healthy confidence of the sun-flushed manliness of his breast—is the silence, the incomprehensible statements that come from it, alone with her, a way of tormenting her? Does he do it only to annoy, to punish? And what has she done to deserve what he doesn't mete out to others? Let him keep it to himself. Take a Valium. Anything. Become a vegetarian. In the heat of the afternoon everyone goes to their rooms or their makeshift beds on the shaded part of the deck, to sleep off the lunchtime wine. Even in the room allotted to them, he keeps up, out of sight of the company (but they are only a wall away, he knows they are there), what is expected. It is so hot he and she have stripped to their briefs. He passes a hand over her damp breasts, gives a lazy sigh, and is asleep on his back. Would he have wanted to take her nipples in his mouth, commit himself to love-making, if he hadn't fallen asleep, or was his a gesture from the wings just in case the audience might catch a glimpse of a slump to an off-stage presence?

The house party is like the fire the servant makes at dusk within the reed stockade beside the lodge. One never knows when a fire outdoors will smoke or take flame cleanly and make a grand blaze, as this one does. One never knows when a small gathering will remain disparate, unresponsive, or when, as this time, men and women will ignite and make a bright company. The ceremony of the evening meal was a bit ridiculous, but perhaps intended as such, and fun. A parody of old colonial times: the stockade against the wild beasts, the black man beating a drum to announce the meal, the chairs placed carefully by him in a missionary prayer-meeting circle well away from the fire, the whisky and wine set out, the smell of charred flesh from the cooking grids. Look up: the first star in the haze is the mast-light of a ship moving out, slipping moorings, breaking with this world. Look down: the blue flames are nothing but burning fat, there are gnawed bones on the swept earth. He's been drinking a lot—she noticed: so that he could stomach it all, no doubt he tells himself.

The fire twitches under ash and the dinner orchestra of insects whose string instruments are their own bodies, legs scraping against legs, wings scraping against carapace, has been silenced by the rising of the moon. But laughter continues. In the huge night, not reduced to scale by buildings, tangled by no pylons and wires, hollowed out by no street- and window-lights into habitable enclosures, the laughter, the voices are vagrant sound that one moment flies right up boldly into space, the next makes a wave so faint it dies out almost as it leaves the lips. Everyone interrupts everyone else, argues, teases. There are moments of acerbity; the grapes they are eating pop into sharp juice as they are bitten. One of the quiet guests has become communicative as will the kind who never risk ideas or opinions of their own but can reproduce, when a subject brings the opportunity, information they have read and stored. Bats; the twirling rags darker against the dark—someone suggested, as a woman cowered, that fear of them comes from the fact that they can't be heard approaching.

'If your eyes are closed, and a bird flies overhead, you'll hear the resistance of air to its wings.'

'And also, you can't make out what a bat's like, where its head is—just a *thing*, ugh!'

The quiet guest was already explaining, no, bats will not bump into you, but not, as this is popularly believed, because they have an inbuilt radar system; their system is sonar, or echolocation—

'—I wear a leopard skin coat!'

The defiant soprano statement from a sub-conversation breaks through his monologue and loses him attention.

It is the pretty girl; she has greased her face against the day's exposure to the sun and her bone-structure elegantly reflects the frail light coming from the half moon, the occasional waver of flame roused in the fire, or the halo of a cigarette lighter. She is almost beautiful. '—D'you hear that!' 'Glynis, where did you find this girl?' 'Shall we put her out to be eaten by her prey, expose her on a rock?'

'No leopards here, unfortunately.'

'The coat would look much better on the leopard than on you.' The wit did not live up to his reputation, merely repeated in sharper, more personal paraphrase what had been well said no one remembered by whom. He spoke directly to the girl, whereas the others were playfully half-indignant around her presence. But the inference, neither entirely conservationist nor aesthetic, seemed to excite the girl's interest in this man. She was aware of him, in the real sense, for the first time.

'Wait till you see me in it.' Just the right touch of independence, hostility.

'That could be arranged.'

This was a sub-exchange, now, under the talk of the others; he was doing the right thing, responding with the innuendo by which men and women acknowledge chemical correspondences stirring between them. And then she said it, was guided to it like a bat, by echolocation or whatever-it-is, something vibrating from the disgusts in him. 'Would you prefer me to wear a sheepskin one? You eat lamb, I suppose?'

It is easy to lose her in the crisscross of talk and laughter, to enter it at some other level and let fall the one on which she took him up. He is drawn elsewhere—there is refuge, maybe, rock to touch in the ex–political prisoner. The prisoner holds the hand of his pale girl with her big nervously-exposed teeth; no beauty, all love. The last place to look for love is in beauty, beauty is only a skin, the creature's own or that of another animal, over what decays. Love is found in prison, this no-beauty has loved him while his body was not present; and he has loved his brothers—he's talking about them, not using the word, but the sense is there so strongly—although they live shut in with their own pails of dirt, he loves even the murderers whose night-long death songs he heard before they were taken to be hanged in the morning.

'Common criminals? In this country? Under laws like ours?'

'Oh yes, we politicals were kept apart, but with time (I was there ten months) we managed to communicate. (There are so many ways you don't think of, outside, when you don't need to.) One of them—young, my age—he was already declared a habitual criminal, inside for an indeterminate sentence. Detention's also an indeterminate sentence, in a way, so I could have some idea . . .'

'You hadn't killed, robbed—he must have done that over and over.'

'Oh he had. But I hadn't been born the bastard of a kitchen maid who had no home but her room in a white woman's back yard, I hadn't been sent to a "homeland" where the woman who was supposed to take care of me was starving and followed her man to a squatter camp in Cape Town to look for work. I hadn't begged in the streets, stolen what I needed to eat, sniffed glue for comfort. He had his first new clothes, his first real bed when he joined a gang of car thieves. Common lot; common criminal.'

Common sob story.

'If he had met you outside prison he would have knifed you for your watch.'

'Possibly! Can you say "That's mine" to people whose land was taken from them by conquest, a gigantic hold-up at the point of imperial guns?'

And the bombs in the streets, in the cars, in the supermarkets, that kill with a moral, necessary end, not criminal intent (yes, to be criminal is to kill for self-gain)—these don't confuse *him*, make carrion of brotherhood. He's brave enough to swallow it. No gagging.

Voices and laughter are cut off. You don't come to the bush to talk politics. It is one of the alert silences called for now and then by someone who's heard, beyond human voices, a cry. *Shhhhh*... Once it was the mean complaining of jackals, and—nearer—a nasal howl from a hyena, that creature of big nostrils made to scent spilt blood. Then a squeal no one could identify: a hare pounced on by a wheeling owl? A warthog attacked by—whom? What's going on, among them, that other order, of the beasts, in their night? 'They live twenty-four hours, we waste the dark.' 'Norbert—you used to be such a nightclub bird!' And the young doctor offers: 'They hunt for their living in shifts, just like us. Some sleep during the day.' 'Oh but they're *designed* as different species, in order to use actively all twenty-four hours. We are one species, designed for daylight only. It's not so many generations since—pre-industrial times, that's all—we went to bed at nightfall. If the world's energy supplies should run out, we'd be back to that. No electricity. No night shifts. There isn't a variety in our species that has night vision.' The bat expert takes up this new cue. 'There are experiments with devices that may provide night vision, they're based on—'

'Shhhhh...'

Laughter like the small explosion of a glass dropped.

'Shut up, Claire!'

All listen, with a glisten of eye movements alone, dead still.

It is difficult for them to decide on what it is they are eavesdropping. A straining that barely becomes a grunt. A belching stir; scuffling, scuffling—but it could be a breeze in dead leaves, it is not the straw crepitation of the reeds at the river, it comes from the other direction, behind the lodge. There is a gathering, another gathering somewhere there. There is communication their ears are not tuned to, their comprehension cannot decode; some event outside theirs. Even the ex–political prisoner does not know what he hears; he who has heard through prison walls, he who has comprehended and decoded so much the others have not. His is only human knowledge, after all; he is not a twenty-four-hour creature, either.

Into this subdued hush breaks the black man jangling a tray of glasses he has washed. The host signals: be quiet, go away, stop fussing among dirty plates. He comes over with the smile of one who knows he has something to offer. 'Lions. They kill one, two maybe. Zebras.'

Everyone bursts the silence like schoolchildren let out of class.

'Where?'

'How does he know?'

'What's he say?'

He keeps them waiting a moment, his hand is raised, palm up, pink from immersion in the washing-up. He is wiping it on his apron. 'My wives hear it, there in my house. Zebra, and now they eating. That side, there, behind.'

The black man's name is too unfamiliar to pronounce. But he is no longer nameless, he is the organizer of an expedition; they pick up a shortened version of the name from their host. Siza has brought the old truck, four-wheel drive, adapted as a large station wagon, from out of its shed next to his house. Everybody is game, this is part of the entertainment the host hoped but certainly could not promise to be lucky enough to provide; all troop by torchlight the hundred yards from the lodge, under the Mopane trees, past the bed of cannas outlined with whitewashed stones (the host never has had the heart to tell Siza this kind of white man's house does not need a white man's kind of garden) to Siza's wives' pumpkin and tomato patch. Siza is repairing a door-handle of the vehicle with a piece of wire, commanding, in his own language, this and that from his family standing by. A little boy gets underfoot and he lifts and dumps him out of the way. Two women wear traditional turbans but the one has a T-shirt with an advertising logo; girl children hang on their arms, jabbering. Boys are quietly jumping with excitement.

Siza's status in this situation is clear when the two wives and children do not see the white party off but climb into the vehicle among them, the dry-soled hard little feet of the children nimbly finding space among the guests' shoes, their knobbly heads with knitted capping of hair unfamiliar to the touch, flesh to flesh, into which all in the vehicle are crowded. Beside the girl with her oiled face and hard slender body perfumed to smell like a lily there is the soft bulk of one of the wives, smelling of woodsmoke. 'Everybody in? Everybody okay?' No, no, wait—someone has gone back for a forgotten flash-bulb. Siza has started up the engine; the whole vehicle jerks and shakes.

Wit is not called for, nor flirtation. He does what is expected: runs to the lodge to fetch a sweater, in case his wife gets chilly. There is barely room for him to squeeze by; she attempts to take a black child on her lap, but the child is too shy. He lowers himself somehow into what space there is. The vehicle moves, all bodies, familiar and unfamiliar, are pressed together, swaying, congealed, breathing in contact. She smiles at him, dipping her head sideways, commenting lightly on the human press, as if he were someone else: 'In for the kill.'

It is not possible to get out.

Everyone will be quite safe if they stay in the car and please roll up the windows, says the host. The headlights of the old vehicle have shown Siza trees like other trees, bushes like other bushes that are, to him, signposts. The blundering of the vehicle through bush and over tree-stumps, anthills, and dongas has been along his highway; he has stopped suddenly, and there they are, shadow-shapes and sudden phosphorescent slits in the dim arch of trees that the limit of the headlights' reach only just creates, as a candle, held up, feebly makes a cave of its own aura. Siza drives with slow-motion rocking and heaving of the human load, steadily nearer. Four shapes come forward along the beams; and stop. He stops. Motes of dust, scraps of leaf and bark knocked off the vegetation float blurring the beams surrounding four lionesses who stand, not ten yards away.

Their eyes are wide, now, gem-yellow, expanded by the glare they face, and never blink. Their jaws hang open and their heads shake with panting, their bodies are bellows expanding and contracting between stiff-hipped haunches and heavy narrow shoulders that support the heads. Their tongues lie exposed, the edges rucked up on either side, like red cloth, by long white incisors.

They are dirtied with blood and to human eyes de-sexed, their kind of femaleness without femininity, their kind of threat and strength out of place, associated with the male. They have no beauty except in the almighty purpose of their stance. There is nothing else in their gaunt faces: nothing but the fact, behind them, of half-grown and younger cubs in the rib-cage of a zebra, pulling and sucking at bloody scraps.

The legs and head are intact in dandyish dress of black and white. The beast has been, is being eaten out. Its innards are missing; the half-digested grasses that were in its stomach have been emptied on the ground, they can be seen—someone points this out in a whisper. But even the undertone is a transgression. The lionesses don't give forth the roar that would make their menace recognizable, something to deal with. Utterances are not the medium for this confrontation. Watching. That is all. The breathing mass, the beating hearts in the vehicle—watching the cubs jostling for places within the cadaver; the breathing mass, the beating hearts in the vehicle—being watched by the lionesses. The beasts have no time, it will be measured by their fill. For the others, time suddenly begins again when the young doctor's girl-friend begins to cry soundlessly and the black children look away from the scene and see the tears shining on her cheeks, and stare at her fear. The young doctor asks to be taken back to the lodge; the compact is broken, people protest, why, oh no, they want to stay and see what happens, one of the lionesses has broken ranks and turns on a greedy cub, cuffing it out of the gouged prey. Quite safe; the car is perfectly safe, don't open a window to photograph. But the doctor is insistent: 'This old truck's chassis is cracked right through, we're overloaded, we could be stuck here all night.'

'Unreal.' Back in the room, the wife comes out with one of the catch-alls that have been emptied of dictionary meaning so that they may fit any experience the speaker won't take the trouble to define. When he doesn't respond she stands a moment, in the doorway, her bedclothes in her arms, smiling, gives her head a little shake to show how overwhelming her impression has been.

Oh well. What can she expect. Why come, anyway? Should have stayed at home. So he doesn't want to sleep in the open, on the deck. Under the stars. All right. No stars, then.

He lies alone and the mosquitoes are waiting for his blood, upside-down on the white board ceiling.

No. Real. *Real.* Alone, he can keep it intact, exactly that: the stasis, the existence without time and without time there is no connection, the state in which he really need have, has no part, could have no part, there in the eyes of the lionesses. Between the beasts and the human load, the void. It is more desired and awful than could ever be conceived; he does not know whether he is sleeping, or dead.

There is still Sunday. The entertainment is not over. Someone has heard lions round the lodge in the middle of the night. The scepticism with which this claim is greeted is quickly disproved when distinct pugs are found in the dust that surrounds the small swimming-pool which, like amniotic fluid, steeps the guests at their own body temperature. The host is not surprised; it has happened before: the lionesses must have come down to quench the thirst their feasting had given them. And the scent of humans, sleeping so near, up on the deck, the sweat of humans in the humid night, their sighs and sleep-noises? Their pleasure- and anxiety-emanating dreams?

'As far as the lions are concerned, we didn't exist.' From the pretty girl, the remark is a half-question that trails off.

'When your stomach is full you don't smell blood.'

The ex-prisoner is perhaps extrapolating into the class war?—the wit puts in, and the ex-prisoner himself is the one who is most appreciatively amused.

After the mosquitoes had had their fill sleep came as indifferently as those other bodily states, hunger and thirst. A good appetite for fresh pawpaw and bacon, boerewors and eggs. Hungry, like everybody else. His wife offers him a second helping, perhaps he needs feeding up, there is a theory that all morbid symptoms are in fact of physical origin. Obsession with injustice—what's wrong with the world is a disease you, an individual, can't cure, that's life. The one who went to prison may be suffering from a lack of something—amino acids, vitamins; or an excess of something, overfeeding when a child or hyperactive thyroid gland. Research is being done.

Siza confirms that the lionesses came to drink. They passed his house; he heard them. He tells this with the dry, knowing smile of one who is aware of a secret to-and-fro between bedrooms. After breakfast he is going to take the party to see in daylight where the kill took place last night.

'But is there anything to see?'

Siza is patient. 'They not eat all. Is too much. So they leave some, tonight they come back for eat finish.'

'No thanks! I don't think we should disturb them again.' But nobody wants the young doctor and his girl-friend to come, anyway, and spoil the outing.

'The lions they sleeping now. They gone away. Come back tonight. Is not there now.'

The wife is watching to see if she and her husband are going along. Yes, he's climbing, limber, into the old vehicle with the cracked chassis, he's giving a hand up to the hostess, he's said something that makes her laugh and purse her mouth.

The black women are thumping washing at an outdoor tub. Neither they nor their children come on this expedition. There is room to breathe without contact, this time. Everything is different in daylight. It is true that the lionesses are absent; the state that he achieved last night is absent in the same way, like them, drugged down by daylight.

Not a lion to be seen. Siza has stopped the vehicle, got out, but waved the passengers to stay put. The scrub forest is quiet, fragile pods that burst and sow their seed by wind-dispersion spiral slowly. Everybody chatters. The stockbroker leaves the vehicle and everybody shouts at him. All right. All right. Taking his time, to show his lack of fear, he climbs aboard. 'Lions are not bulls and bears, Fred.' They laugh at this mild jeer which is the kind expected to sustain the wit's image—all are amused except the stockbroker himself, who knows the remark, in turn, refers to his image of himself as one whom no one would guess to be a stockbroker.

Siza comes back and beckons. The vehicle is quickly quit. And now the emptiness of the scrub forest is untrustworthy, all around, you can't see what's behind dead brush, fallen logs and the screens of layered branches that confine vision to ten feet. They talk only softly, in the sense of being stalked. The black man is leading them along what looks almost like a swept path; but it has been swept by a large body being dragged through dust and dead leaves: there is the carcass of the zebra, half-hidden in a thicket.

'No tyre-tracks, we didn't drive right into here! This can't be the place.'

'They pull him here for when they come back tonight.'

'What! To keep the meat fresh?'

'For the birds mustn't see.' Siza gives a name in his language.

'He means vultures. Vultures, eh, Siza.' A mime of the vultures' hunched posture.

'Yes, those big birds. Come look here—' The tour continues, he takes them a few paces from the carcass and stands beside a mound over which earth has been scratched or kicked. Flies whose backs spark tinny green and gold are settled on it. The black man has his audience: taking up a stick, he prods the mound and it stirs under dust like flour-coated meat moved by a fork.

'Christ, the intestines! Look at the size of that liver or spleen!'

'You mean lions can do that? Store things covered? How do they do it, just with their paws?'

'It's exactly the way my cat covers its business in the garden, scratches up earth. They're cats, too.'

The young jailbird and his girl and the antique dealer have made a discovery for themselves, having, in the confidence of excitement, retraced for a short distance the way along which the kill was approached. They have found the very pile of the contents of the zebra's stomach that someone noticed last night.

It is another mound. He has come over from the mound of guts they are marvelling at. There is nothing to watch in dead flesh, it is prodded and it falls back and is still. But this mound of steaming grass that smells sweetly of cud (it has been heated by the sun as it was once heated by the body that contained it) is not dead to human perception. What's going on here is a visible transformation of an inert mass. It is literally being carried away by distinctly different species of beetles who know how to live by decay, the waste of the digestive tract. The scarabs with their armoured heads burrow right into the base of the mound, and come out backwards, rolling their ball of dung between their strong, tined legs. The tunnels they have mined collapse and spread the mound more thinly on its periphery; smaller beetles are flying in steadily to settle there, where their lighter equipment can function. They fly away carrying their appropriate load in a sac—or between their front legs, he can't quite make out. A third species, middle-sized but with a noisy buzz, function like helicopters, hovering and scooping off the top of the mound. They are flattening it perfectly evenly, who can say how or why they bother with form? That's life. If every beetle has its place, how is refusal possible. And if refusal is possible, what place is there. No question mark. These are statements. That is why there is no point in making them to anyone. There is no possible response.

The mound is slowly going to disappear; maybe the vehicle is about to take the party back to the lodge, the weekend is going to be over. He is walking back to the rest of the party, still gathered round the carcass and the black man. For the space of a few yards he is alone, for a few seconds he is equidistant between those at the dung mound and those up ahead, part of neither one nor the other. A sensation that can't be held long; now he is with the group at the kill, again. There is some special stir of attentiveness in them, they crowd round and then herd back a step, where Siza, the black man, is crouched on his hunkers. He is business-like, concentrated, not taking any notice of them. He has given them all he could; now he has the air of being for himself. He has a knife in his hand and the white man who has just joined the group recognizes it, it is the knife that is everywhere, nowhere without the knife, on the news, at the dark street-corners, under the light that the warders never turn out. The black man has thrust, made his incision, sliced back the black-and-white smooth pelt on the dead beast's uppermost hind leg and now is cutting a piece of the plump rump. It is not a chunk or hunk, but neatly butchered, prime—a portion.

They laugh, wondering at the skill, curious. As if they can't guess, as if they've never sunk their teeth into a steak in their lives. 'What're you going to do with that, Siza?' Ah yes, put it in a doggy bag, take it home when you've already stuffed your own guts, taken the land (as the jailbird would say).

The black man is trimming it. Along with the knife, he has brought a sheet of newspaper. 'For me. Eat it at my house. For my house.'

'Is it good meat?'

'Yes, it's good.'

One of the men chides, man to man. 'But why not take the whole haunch—the whole leg, Siza. Why such a small piece?'

The black man is wrapping the portion in newspaper, he knows he mustn't let it drip blood on the white people.

He does it to his satisfaction in his own time and looks up at them. 'The lions, they know I must take a piece for me because I find where their meat is. They know it. It's all right. But if I take too much, they know it also. Then they will take one of my children.'

Safe Houses

He's one of those dark-haired men whose beards grow out rusty-red. He could have dyed his hair to match—more or less—but a beard is the first thing they'd expect to find you behind. He's lived like this several times before; the only difference is that this time he came back into the country legally, came home—so much for the indemnity promised to exiles, so much for the changed era there, now bans on his kind of politics were supposed to be a thing of the past, he was supposed to be—free? He knows how their minds work—not much imagination, reliance on an Identikit compilation of how political subversives look and behave Underground. Underground: this time, as at other times, he's aware of how unsuitably abstract a term that is. To hide away, you have to be out in the open of life; too soon and easily run to ground, holed up somewhere. Best safety lies in crowds. Selective crowds; he goes to football matches with beer in a knapsack, and a cap with a plastic eyeshade over his sunglasses, but not to pop concerts, where the police keep an eye on young leftists whose democratic recreation this is. He goes to the movies but not to concerts although he longs for the company of strings and brass; someone among his intellectual buddies from long ago would be bound to gaze at him, reaching back for recognition. Small gatherings where everyone can be trusted are traps; glowing with the distinction of the secret encounter with a real revolutionary, someone will not be able to resist boasting to another, in strictest confidence, and that other will pass on the luminous dusting of danger.

The good friends who provide a bed sometimes offer the use of a car as well, but driving alone is another sure way to be traced and picked up. He walks, and takes buses among ordinary workers and students. He's a little too forty-five-ish, thickened around the jowl and diaphragm, to pass as a student but with his cravat of tangled black hair showing in the neck of a sweat shirt and his observance of the uniform jogging shoes with soles cushioned like tyres, he could be anyone among the passengers—the white artisans, railway and post office employees, even policemen. Reading a newspaper with its daily account of the proceedings at the group trial where he is a missing accused, worrying about these comrades in arms, he tries not to feel self-congratulatory at his escape of arrest, a form of complacency dangerous to one in his position, sitting there in a bus among people he knows would be glad to hand him over to the law; but he can't suppress a little thrill, a sort of inner giggle. Perhaps *this* is freedom? Something secret, internal, after all? But philosophizing is another danger, in his situation, undermining the concept of freedom for which he has risked discovery and imprisonment yet again.

One afternoon in the city he was gazing inattentively out of the window waiting for the bus to set off when he became aware of the presence just seating itself beside him. Aware like an animal: scenting something different in the bus's familiar sun-fug of sweat and deodorants, fruit-skins and feet. Perfume. Real perfume, at the price of a month's wages of the other passengers. And a sound, a sound of silk as a leg crossed the knee of another leg. He straightened away from the window, looked ahead for a decent interval and then slowly turned, as if merely fidgeting because the bus was taking too long to leave.

A woman, of course—he'd scented that. Grey silk pants or some sort of fashionable skirt divided like pants, with an arched instep showing in a pastel sandal. Below the neck-line of a loose blouse, silk slopes shining—breasts rising and falling. Out of breath. Or exasperated. He moved a little to give her more room. She nodded in acknowledgement without looking at him; she didn't see him, she was going through some sort of dialogue or more likely mon-ologue in her head, annoyance, exasperation twitched her lips.

Schoolgirls tramped onto the bus with their adolescent female odours and the pop of gum blown between their lips like the text balloons in comics. An old woman opened a bag of vinegary chips. The bus filled but the driver was absent.

This misplaced person, this woman, this pampered almost-beauty (he saw as she turned, throwing back her long, tiger-streaked hair cut in a parrot-poll over the fore-head, and smiling on perfectly conformed teeth) had now accepted where she found herself. She indicated the driver's seat. —What d'you think's happened to him?—

Taking a leak. —Having a cup of coffee, I suppose.—
They shared the polite moment of tolerance.

—I thought they had a strict timetable. Oh well. D'you
know if this takes us along Sylvia Pass?—

—Pretty near the top of the Pass.—

She pulled a face and blinked her thick-lashed eyes in
resigned dismay. Secretive, glossy eyes, knowing how to
please, and folding at the outer corners an attractive, ex-
perienced fan of faint lines.

—Where do you want to get off?—

—That's the problem—at the bottom of the Pass. I suppose I should have taken some other bus . . . I don't know
why taxis don't cruise in this town as they do in any other
civilized place! I've been looking for one for half an hour,
traipsing . . . —

—There should have been taxis for tourists at any hotel.—

—No, no, I live here, but this just isn't my day . . . my car's
stuck in a parking garage. Underground. Infuriating. Bat-
tery dead or something. I couldn't find a telephone booth
where the receiver hadn't been torn out . . . this town! I had
to ask a shopkeeper to let me phone for a mechanic . . .
anyway, I couldn't wait any longer, I've left the keys with
the attendant.—

She felt better now that she had told someone, anyone.
He was anyone.

When the driver appeared and fares were to be paid of
course she had neither season card nor change for a ticket.
While she scrabbled in her bag, gold chains on her wrists
sliding, he gave the conductor two tickets.

—Oh you are kind . . . — She was suddenly embarrassed
by her privileged life, by her inability to cope with what for
all the people surrounding her on the bus was daily routine.
In their ignoring of her she felt a reproach that she had

never travelled on the bus before, perhaps not this bus or any bus, at least since she was a schoolchild. He was no longer *anyone*; somehow an ally, although from his appearance he probably could ill afford to waste a bus ticket on a stranger. Yet there was something in his self-assurance, the amusement in his regard, that suggested he was not merely one of the other passengers. Unsure of this, in a habit of patronage—she was the kind who would treat her servants generously but send her children to segregated schools—she chattered to him to show she considered him an equal. —You make the journey every day? Isn't it always bliss to get home, out of this town?—

—Every day, no. But what's wrong with the city?— Too full of blacks for you, now, lady, blacks selling fruit and cheap jewellery and knitted caps, dirtying the streets, too full of men without work for whom you see your bracelets and that swish Italian suède bag as something to be taken from you.

She shifted to safe generalization. —Oh I'm no city girl. Not anywhere.—

—But you live in one?—

—Well, you'd hardly know it was there, from my house. Luckily. It's an old suburb...the trees—that's one thing about Johannesburg, isn't it, you can hide yourself in trees, just the highways humming, well out of sight!—

—Really?— He suddenly gave way in a great, open smile like the yawn of a predator.

She had the instinct to withdraw. —You don't live here?—

—Oh yes, I'm living here.—

She suppressed her casual curiosity as unwise encouragement. —Could you tell me when to get off? The nearest stop to Sylvia Pass.—

She did not know if she imagined a pause.

—I'll be getting off there.—

He stood behind her as she stepped down from the bus. They began to descend the steep and winding road. There was no distance between them but an aura which established they were not together, merely taking the same route. —Thank God it's down and not up. My heels are not exactly appropriate for this.—

—Take them off. It's safer. The surface is very smooth.—

—But it's hot! I'll burn my feet.—

She clattered along awkwardly, amused at her own manner of progress. —Isn't it typical? I've been jogging around here every morning for years and I've never come down the Pass before.—

—It would be up the Pass, wouldn't it—if you live at the bottom. Quite a strenuous jog.— An observation rather than a correction. And then: —Typical of what?—

None of his business! Who was he to quiz a manner of speaking, as if to find out if it had some significance in her life.

Yet she attempted an answer. —Oh . . . habit, I suppose . . . doing what you've become used to, not noticing . . . where you really are—

And wondering, now, no doubt, whether it was possible that this man off the bus really could be living in the suburb of large houses hidden by trees where she lived, or whether he had left the bus to follow her, and was to be feared, although he was white, in this city where so much was to be feared. It was true that he had picked one of his maze of trails about the city and suburbs in order to walk with her—an impulse like any of the impulses with which he had to fill in the days of his disconnection from consecutive action. The unexpected was his means of survival. To be Underground is to have a go at living without consequences.

The corrupt little wriggle of freedom—there it was again. Shameful but enjoyable.

—Here's my corner.— She bent to pull the slipped strap of her sandal back over her heel and looked up ingratiatingly to soften dismissal.

—Goodbye then.— Again, that greedy warrior's smile, contradicting the humble appearance.

As he turned his back she suddenly called as she might have remembered an instruction for some tradesman —Have you far to go—that was such a hot trek—would you like to come in for something cool to drink?—

This time she was not mistaken; there was a pause, still with his back to her. —I know I'm dying of thirst and you must be!—

So she drew him round, and murmuring casual thanks, he joined her. Now they were walking together. At one of the pillared entrances in white battlements topped with black iron spikes she pressed the button of an intercom panel and spoke. The flats of a stage set, the wide polished wooden gates slid back electronically. Trees, her trees led up to and overflowed the roof of the spread wings of the house. Small dogs jumped about her. Sprinklers arched rainbows over lawns. She called out in the joyous soprano used to summon faithful servants, and ice and fruit juice were brought onto a shaded terrace. Behind him the colours of Persian carpets, paintings and bowls of flowers blurred in the deep perspective of one of those huge rooms used for parties.

—You have a lovely home.— He said what was blandly expected of him as he drank juice in return for a bus ticket.

She came back with what was expected of her. —But too big. My sons are at boarding school. For two people...too much.—

—But the garden, the privacy.—

She was embarrassed to think how he must be envying her. —Oh yes. But most of the time I don't use the rest of the place (a gesture to the room behind), I have my own little quarters on the other side of the house. My husband's away such a lot on business—Japan, at the moment. That's why I couldn't even get anyone to come and fetch me from that wretched garage . . . his secretary's such an idiot, she's let his driver go. I always tell him, he's drained her of all initiative, she's so used to being ordered about. I can't stand subservient people, can you—I mean, I want to shake them and get them to *stand up*—

—I don't think I know any.—

—Ah, that shows you move in the right circles!— They both laughed. —But what do you do? Your profession, your work, I mean.— Careful to show that 'work' might be just as worthy as a profession.

Without realizing he could think so quickly, he began inventing one—a profession combined with 'work'—that would fit his appearance, he began telling like a fairy tale, a bedtime story, it flowed from him taking turns and details as if it could be true, as if he were making an alternative life for himself: —I'm in construction. Construction engineer—that's where I was today, on some sites. Things go wrong . . . when you're talking about stress in a twenty-storey building—

—Oh if it were to fall! I often look up and marvel how such piles hold together, in fact I don't have much faith they will, I never walk under those pavement shelters you people erect for pedestrians while you're building, I always walk in the street, I'd rather get run over, any time—

—Standards are pretty high, here; safety margins. You don't have to worry. In some of the countries I've worked, it's rather different. And one has always to think of how a construction will behave in an earthquake, how do you build over a fault in the earth, Mexico City, San Francisco—

—So you travel around, too. But not selling; building.—

—Sometimes pulling down. Preparing to rebuild. Destroying old structures.— No—he must resist the devilry of amusing himself by planting, in his fairy tale, symbols from his real life. As in all fairy tales, there were enough improbabilities his listener would have to pass over if not swallow. It surely must occur to her that a construction engineer would be unlikely not to utilize his own car, even if his working garb was appropriate to inspection of building sites. —Have you travelled much with your husband? Go along with him?— Best to know where she had been before elaborating on projects in Sri Lanka, Thailand, North Africa. No, she liked to go to Europe but hot places, crowded places, dirty places—no.

So he was free to transform his experience of guerrilla training camps in Tanzania and Libya, his presence in the offices of an exiled High Command in cities deadened by northern snows or tropical heat, to provide exotic backdrops for his skyscrapers. Anecdotes of bar encounters in such places—he merely changed the subjects discussed, not the characters—entertained her. He was at ease in his invented persona; what would a woman know about engineering? She said it was time for a real drink; ice was brought again, a trolley was wheeled out in which bottles were slotted, a manservant appeared with a dish of snacks decorated with radish roses.

—I don't allow myself to drink on my own.—

—Why not?— He accepted the glass of whisky and ice she had prepared for him.

At first she seemed not to hear the personal question,

busying herself at the trolley. She sat down on a swinging sofa, holding her drink, and let the sandals drop from her feet. —Afraid.—

—Of being alone?—

—No. Of carrying on with it. Yes, of being alone. Isn't that why people drink—I mean really drink. But I suppose you're often alone.—

—What makes you think that?—

But now it was he who need not be afraid: she had no inkling of anything real behind his fairy tales. —Well, the nature of your work—always moving around, no time for roots.—

—No trees.— He lifted his shoulders, culpable.

—What about family . . . —

Should he have a family? —Dispersed. I don't have what you'd call a family, really.—

—Your wife? No children?—

—I had one once—a wife. I have a grown-up daughter— in Canada. A doctor, a paediatrician, bright girl.—

That was a mistake. —Oh where? I have a brother who emigrated to Canada, he's a doctor too, also a paediatrician, in Toronto.—

—Vancouver. She's the other side of the country.—

—They might have met at some conference. Doctors are always holding conferences. What's her name— She held out her hand to take his glass for a refill, gesturing him to be at ease. —Good lord, I haven't asked you yours—I'm, well, I'm Sylvie, Sylvie—

—That's enough. I'm Harry.—

—Well, maybe you're right—that's enough.— For some-one met on a bus, when you haven't travelled on a bus for, say, thirty years; she laughed with the acknowledgement to herself.

—I'll leave you my card if you wish.— (His card!) They were both laughing.

—I'm unlikely to need the services of a construction engineer.—

—Your husband might.— He was enjoying his recklessness, teasing himself.

She put down her drink, crossed her arms and began to swing, like a child wanting to go higher and higher. The couch squeaked and she frowned sideways, comically. The whisky made her lips fuller and polished her eyes. —And how would I explain I got to know you, may I ask.—

Re-establishing reserve, almost prim, he ended the repartee. When he had emptied his glass he rose to leave. —I've imposed upon you too long...—

—No...no...— She stood up, hands dangling at her sides, bracelets slipping. —I hope you're refreshed...I certainly am.— She pressed the button that opened her fortress and saw him to the gates. —Maybe—I don't know, if you're not too busy—maybe you'd like to come round sometime. Lunch, or a swim. I could ring you—

—Thank you.—

—When my husband is back.—

She gazed straight at him; as if he were an inferior reminded of his manners he produced a thank you, once more.

—Where can I reach you? Your phone—

He, who could pass a police station without crossing to the other side of the street, tingled all the way up from his feet. Caught. —Well, it's awkward...messages...I'm hardly ever in—

Her gaze changed; now she was the one who was put in her place. —Oh. Well drop by sometime. Anyway, it was nice meeting you. You might as well take my number—

He could not refuse. He found a ballpoint in his trouser pocket but no paper. He turned his left hand palm up and wrote the seven digits across the veins showing on the vulnerable inner side of his wrist.

The number was a frivolous travesty of the brand concentration-camp survivors keep of their persecution; he noticed that when he got back to the house that was sheltering him at the time. He washed off her identification; it required the use of his hosts' nailbrush. The Movement wanted him to slip out of the country but he resisted the pressures that reached him. He had been in exile too long to go back to that state of being, once he had come home. Home? Yes, even sleeping on the floor in somebody's kitchen (his standard of shelter was extremely varied), going to football matches, banal movies, wandering the streets among the people to whom he knew he belonged, unrecognized, unacknowledged—that was home. He read every newspaper and had the rare events of carefully-arranged clandestine meetings with people in the Movement, but these were too risky for both himself and them for this to happen often. He thought of writing something; he actually had been an academic once, long ago, another life, teaching the laws that he despised. But it was unwise to have bits of paper around you, anything written down was evidence of your existence, and his whole strategy was not to exist, for the time being, in any persona of his past or present. For the first time in his life he was bored. He ate peanuts, biscuits, biltong, buying these small sealed packets and tearing them open, tossing the contents from his palm into his mouth before he'd even left the shop, as he had done when he was an overweight schoolboy. Although he walked the streets, he had thickened, rounding into that mound under the diaphragm. Whatever he thought of to fill the days and nights, he stopped short of doing; either it would involve people who would be afraid to associate with him, or would endanger those who would risk it. Oddly, after more than a week the phone number came back to him at the sight of his own inner wrist as he fastened his watchstrap. Sylvie—what was her name? Sylvie. Just that. Sylvie, Sylvia Pass. Perhaps the name was also the invention of the moment, out of caution, self-protection, as his 'Harry' had been. *May I speak to Sylvie? Who? I'm afraid you've got the wrong number*—it would be the husband's voice. And so she never had done anything stupid like picking up a man on a bus.

But from the point of view of his situation if anyone was safe this 'Sylvie' was. He went to the telephone in the silent empty house, his present precarious shelter, from which everyone else had gone to work for the day. She herself answered. She did not sound surprised; he asked if he might take up her offer of a swim. —But of course. After work?— Of course—after he'd left the dust and heat of the building sites.

She was dressed to swim, the strap of a two-piece suit showing above the neck of some loose-flowing robe, and the ridge of the bikini pants outlined under the cloth somewhere below where her navel must be. But she did not swim; she sat smiling, with the thigh-high split in the robe tucked closed round her leg and watched him as he emerged from the chintzy rustic change-room (my god, what luxury compared with his present sleeping quarters) and stalked down to the pool holding in his belly and conscious that this effort—with that diaphragm bulge—made him strut like a randy pigeon. She gave encouraging cries when he dived, he felt she was counting the lengths he did, backstroke, butterfly, crawl. He was irritated and broke water right at her bare feet with his greedy grin of a man snatching life on the run. He must not let that grin escape him too often. She wiggled her toes as water flew from him, his dripping pelt of chest hair, the runnels off his strong legs, spattering her feet. A towel big as a sheet provided a toga for him; wrapped in his chair, he was modestly protected as she was, whether or not she had sized him up like a haunch in a butcher's shop.

The whisky and ice were wheeled out. The kitchen was forewarned this time; there were olives and salami, linen napkins. —Am I going to meet your husband before I go?— The man surely would be driving up any minute. It would be best for 'Harry' to get out of the towel and into his clothes in order to seem the stranger he was. He wanted to ask how she had decided to explain his presence, since she must, indeed, have so decided. The question was in his face although he didn't come out with it. It suddenly seemed impatiently simple to him. Why not just say they'd met in a bus, what was there to hide—or were the circumstances of the casual acquaintance indeed too proletarian for the gentleman, beneath his wife's dignity! If only they'd met in the Members' Pavilion at the races, now!

—Not here.— It was brusque. —It was necessary to go to Hong Kong after Japan. Apparently opportunities are opening up there . . . I don't know what it's all about. And then to Australia.—

—Quite a trip.—

—So long as he's back by the time the boys come home for the holidays at the end of next month. They expect to do things together with him. Fishing trips. Things I'm no good at. You've got a daughter—lucky. I go along, but just for the ride.—

—Well, I'm sorry—

—Another time. But you're not going...you'll stay for dinner. Just something light, out here, such a lovely evening.—

—But haven't you other plans I'd be disturbing, friends coming?— Harry cannot attend dinner parties, thank you.

—Nothing. Not-a-thing. I'm planning an early night, I've been gadding too much. You know how friends imagine, when you're alone, you can't be left to yourself for a single evening. I'm sick of them.—

—Then I should push off and leave you in peace.—

—No, just a salad, whatever they've got—you'll share pot luck—

Sick of them. A cure for boredom: hers. The paradox, rather than her company, was his enjoyment. He accepted the role so wide of his range; he opened the bottles of white wine—dry with the fish mousse, a Sauternes with the strawberries—in place of the man of the house.

Her fascination with their encounter rose to the surface in the ease over food and drink. —How many years is it since you met anyone you were not introduced to—can you remember? I certainly can't. It's a chain, isn't it, it's like Auld Lang Syne all the year, every year, it just goes on and on, a hand on this side taken by a hand on that side...it's never broken into, always friends of friends, acquaintances of acquaintances, whether they're from Japan or Taiwan or London, down the road or god knows where.—

—Good friends. They're necessary.— He was careful.

—But don't you find that? Particularly for people like you and him—my husband—I mean, the circle of people who have particular business interests, a profession. Round and round . . . But I suppose it's natural for us because we have things in common. I thought, that other day—when my car broke down, you know—I never walk around the streets like this, what have all these people to do with me—

It was coming now, of course, the guilt of her class in a wail of self-accusation of uselessness, of not belonging to real life. Hadn't she shown a hint of it in the bus? But he was wrong and, in his turn, fascinated by the overturning of his kind of conventional assumption.

—They're unreal to me. I don't just mean because most of them are black. That's obvious, that we have nothing in common. I wish them well, they ought to have a better life . . . conditions . . . I suppose it's good that things are changing for them . . . but I'm not involved, how could I be, we give money for their schools and housing and so on— my husband's firm does, like everybody else . . . I suppose you too . . . I don't know what your views are—

—I'm no armchair politician.—

—I thought not. But the others—what have I in common with those whites, either . . . I don't count in their life, and they don't count in mine. And the few who might—who're hidden away in the crowd in those streets (why is this town so ugly and dirty), it's unlikely I'd recognize them.— She really was quite attractive, unaware of a crumb at the side of her mouth. —Even sitting next to me in a bus.—

They laughed and she made the move to clink glasses.

A black man in white uniform and cotton gloves hung about wearily; her guest was conscious of this witness to everything that went on in whites' houses, but for once felt that his own whiteness guaranteed anonymity. She told the servant he could leave the table and clear it in the morning. Frog bassoons and fluting crickets filled comfortable silences. —I must go.— He spoke, not moving.

—What about a quick dip first. One for the road.— Although he had dressed, she had eaten dinner in her robe.

He was not eager to get into water again but it was a way of rounding off the evening and he felt there was a need for doing this definitively, for himself. There were too few safe subjects between them—she was more right than she knew—they had too little in common, the acquaintance had come to the end of its possibilities. He went to the change-room again.

The water crept like a cool hand over his genitals; she was already swimming. She doubled up and went under with a porpoise flip, and the light from the terrace streamed off her firm backside and thighs. She kept her distance in the water, they circled one another. Hitching herself out on long arms, she sat on the side of the pool and, again, he was aware of her watching him. He surfaced below where she sat, and suddenly, for a moment only, closed his hand on her wrist before leaving the pool, shaking himself like a dog, scrubbing at his arms and chest with the big towel. —Cold, cold.—

She repeated with a mock shiver: —Cold, cold.—

They stood up, in accord to get dressed.

The ring of water in his ears jinglingly mingled with the sound of the frogs. He put his arms round her and in a rush of heat, as if all the blood in his chilled body had retreated to engorge there, pressed his genitals tightly against her. He felt an enormous thrill and a fiercely crashing desire, all the abstinence of a planned nonexistence imploded like the destruction of one of his imaginary twenty-storeys that she feared might fall on her head. She held him as he held her. There was no kiss. She broke away neatly and ran indoors. He dressed, raged against by his roused body, among the chintz drapings in the change-room. When he came out the water in the pool was black, with the reflection of stars thrown there like dying matches. She had turned off the terrace lights and was standing in the dark.

—Good night. I apologize.—

—I hope your car hasn't been pinched. Should have brought it into the drive.—

—There is no car.—

He was too tired and dispirited to lie. Yet he must summon some slapdash resource of protection. —Friends were coming this way, they dropped me. I said I'd call a taxi to take me back.—

The dark and the cover of chanting frogs hid whatever she might be thinking.

—Stay.— She turned, and he followed her into the house, that he had not before entered.

They began again, the right way, with kisses and caresses. A woman his own age, who knew how to make love, who both responded and initiated, knowing what they wanted; in common. On this territory between them, there was even a kind of unexpected bluntness. Gently pinching his nipples before the second intercourse, she said—You're not Aids positive, are you.—

He put a hand over the delight of her fingers on him. —A bit late to ask . . . Not so far as I know. And I've no reason to believe otherwise.—

—But you've no wife.—

—Yes, but I'm rather a constant character—despite my nomadic profession.—

—How will you explain you didn't come home.—

He laughed. —Who to?—

—The first day you were here . . . 'awkward', you said, for me to phone you.—

—There's no one. There's no woman I'm accountable to at present.—

—You understand, it's none of my business. But we don't want to make things difficult for either of us.—

The husband. —Of course, I understand, don't worry. You're a lovely—preposterous!—woman.— And he began to kiss her as if he were a cannibal tasting flesh.

She was a practical woman, too. Some time in the early hours he stirred with a grunt and found a strange woman standing over him in dawn shadows—oh yes, 'Sylvie'. So that's where, waking often in unfamiliar rooms, he was this time. He had learnt to be quick to adjust his sense of place.

—Come. There's another bed.— He wandered behind her down a passage. She had made up a big bed in a guest-room; he stumbled into it and slept again.

In the morning at breakfast on her terrace she gaily greeted the black man who served them. —Mr Harry is a friend of the master, I asked him to stay the night with us.—

So she, too, had the skills of vigilance, making safe for herself.

Harry went back every night that week. Harry really existed, now, out of the nonexistence of himself. Harry the construction engineer, a successful, highly-paid, professionally well-regarded man of the world, with a passing fancy, a mistress not young but beautiful, a creature lavished by the perfumed unguents of care from the poll of curly tendrils he would lift to expose her forehead, to the painted nails of her pedicured toes. Like him, she had her erratic moments of anguish, caused by conflict with the assertion of reality—her reality—rising within her to spoil an episode outside her life, a state without consequences. These moments found their expression as non sequitur remarks or more often as gestures, the inner scuffle breaking through in some odd physical manifestation. One night she squatted naked on the bed with her arms round her knees, clasping her curled feet tight in either hand. He was disturbed, and suppressed the reason that was sending a sucker from the root of his life: after interrogation in detention he had sat on the floor of his cell holding his feet like that, still rigid with his resistance against pain. A sear of resentment: *she*—she was only interrogating herself. Yet of course he had feeling for her—hadn't he just made love to her, and she to him, as she did so generously—he should not let himself dismiss the relative sufferings of people like her as entirely trivial because it was on behalf of nothing larger than themselves.

—A long phone call from Australia...and all I could think about while we were talking was how when we're alone in here at night he never closes the bathroom door while he pees. I hear him, like a horse letting go in the street. Never closes the door. And sometimes there's a loud fart as well. He never stops to think that I can hear, that I'm lying here. And that's all I could think about while he's talking to me, that's all.—

He smiled at her almost fondly. —Well, we're pretty

crude, we men ... but oh come on, you're not squeamish—
you're a very physical lady—

—About love-making, yes ... you think, because of the
things I do, with you. But that's different, that's love-
making, it's got nothing to do with what I'm talking about.—

—If sex doesn't disgust you as a function of the body,
then why so fastidious about its other functions? You accept
a lover's body or you don't.—

—Would you still accept your lover's body if she had,
say, a breast off?—

He lay down beside her with a hand on the dune of her
curved smooth back. —How do I know? What woman?
When? It would depend on many things, wouldn't it? I
can say now, *yes*, just to say the right thing, if you want—

—That's it! That's what's good! You don't say the right
thing, like other people.—

—Oh I do, I do. I'm very careful, I have a wary nature,
I assure you.—

—Well, I don't know you.— She let go of her feet and
pulled the bow of her body back, under his palm. Rest-
lessly she swiveled round to him pushing the fingers of
her two hands up through the poll on her forehead, holding the hair dragged away. —Why do I let that bloody
pansy hairdresser do this to me ... I look common. Cheap,
common.—

He murmured intimately. —I didn't think so.—

On the bus, yes. —Maybe you wouldn't have got off if I
hadn't looked like this. Where were you really going, I
wonder.— But it was not a question; she was satisfied she
wouldn't get an answer, he wouldn't come out with the
right thing. She was not asking, just as she never questioned
that he appeared as out of nowhere, every night, apparently

dropped by taxi somewhere out of sight of the house. And
he did not ask when the husband would come home; there
would be a sign he would read for himself. Stretched out,
she quietly took the hand that had been on her back and
placed it between her thighs.

There was no sign, but at the end of that week he knew
he would not go back again. Enough. It was time. He left
as he had followed her, without explanation. Using the
same trail for more than a week, he might have made a
path for himself by which he could be followed. He moved
from where he had been staying, to be taken in at another
house. This was the family of a plumber, a friend of the
Movement, not quite white, but too ambiguous of pigment
for classification, so that the itinerant lodger could pass for
a lighter relative. One of the youngsters gave up his bed;
the lodger shared the room with three other children. Every
day of the trial, new evidence brought by the Prosecutor's
state witnesses involved his name. It claimed him from every
newspaper, citing several aliases under which he had been
active. But not 'Harry'.

He was making his way back to the plumber's house one
afternoon when the youngster, on roller skates, zigzagged
up the street. The boy staggered to a halt, almost knocking
him down, and he struck out playfully at him. But the boy
was panting. —My dad says don't come. I been waiting to
tell you and my brother's there at the other end of the street
in case you take that way. Dad send us. They come this
morning and went all over the house, only Auntie was there,
Ma was also at work already. Looking for you. With dogs
and everything. He say don't worry for your things, he's

going to bring them where you can pick them up—he didn't tell me nothing, not where, but that you know—

A cold jump of fear under his pectorals. He let it pass, and concentrated on getting out of the area. He took a bus, and another bus. He went into a cinema and sat through some film about three men bringing up a baby. When he came out of the cinema's eternal dusk, the street was dark. Somewhere to go for the night: he had to have that, to decide where to go tomorrow, which hide on the list in his mind it was possible to use again. Likely that the list was not in his mind alone; nothing on it was left that could be counted on as safe, now.

He got out of the taxi a block away. He pressed the intercom button at the wide teak gates. There was the man-servant's accented voice on the other end.

—It's Mr Harry.—

—Just push, Mr Harry.— There was a buzz.

Her trees, the swimming-pool; he stood in the large room that was always waiting for a party to fill it. On low tables were the toys such people give each other: metal balls that (as he set them in motion with a flick) click together in illustration of some mathematical or physical principle, god knows what... Click-clack; a metronome of trivial time. She was there, in the doorway, in rumpled white trousers, barefoot, a woman who expected no one or perhaps was about to choose what she would wear for an evening out.

—Hul-*lo*.— Raised eyebrows.

—I had to go away unexpectedly—trouble with the foundations on one of our sites in Natal. I meant to phone—

—But phoning's awkward.— She recalled, but quite serenely, only half-wishing to score against him.

—I'm not disturbing you...—

—No, no. I've just been tidying up...some cupboards ...I get very careless—

When alone: so the husband wasn't back yet. —Could I ask for a drink—I've had a heavy day.—

She opened her palms, away from her body: as if he need ask; and, indeed, the servant appeared with the trolley. —I put it outside, madam?—

Quite like coming home; the two of them settled back on the terrace, as before. —I thought it would be so nice to see you.—

She had dropped ice in his drink and was handing it to him. —It is nice.—

He closed his fingers round hers, on the glass.

After they had eaten, she asked—Are you going to stay? Just for tonight.—

They were silent a few moments, to the accompaniment of those same frogs. —I feel I'd like to very much.— It was sincere, strangely; he was aware of a tender desire for her, pushing out of mind fear that this, too, was an old trail that might be followed, and awareness that his presence was just a pause in which tomorrow's decision must be made. —And what about you.—

—Yes, I'd like you to. D'you want to swim—

—Not much.—

—Well it's maybe a bit chilly.—

When the servant came to clear the table she gave an order. —Ask Leah please to make up the bed in the first guest-room, will you. For Mr Harry.—

Lying side by side on long chairs in the dark, he stroked her arm and drew back her hair from her shoulder to kiss her neck. She stood up and, taking his hand, led him indeed to that room and not her own. So that was how it was to

be; he said nothing, kissed her on the forehead in acceptance that this was the appropriate way for him to be dismissed with a polite good night. But after he had got naked
into bed she came in, naked, drew back the curtains and
opened the windows so that the fresh night blew in upon
them; and lay down beside him. Their flesh crept deliciously
under the double contact of the breeze and each other's
warmth. There was great tenderness, which perhaps
prompted her to remark, with languid frankness, on a contrast: —You know you were awful, that first day, the way
you just thrust yourself against me. Not a touch, not a kiss.—
Now between a sudden change to wild kisses he challenged
her knowingly. —And you, you, you didn't mind, ay, you
showed no objection...You were not insulted! But was I
really so crude—did I really...?—

—You certainly did. And no other man I know—

—And any other woman would have pushed me into the
swimming-pool.—

They embraced joyously again and again; she could feel
that he had not been with 'any other woman', wherever it
was he had disappeared to after last week. In the middle
of the night, each knew the other had wakened and was
looking at the blur of sinking stars through the open windows. He was sure, for no logical reason, that he was safe,
this night, that no one would know, ever, that he was here.
She suddenly raised herself on one elbow, turning to him
although she certainly could not read his face in the faint
powdering of light from the sky. —Who are you?—

But he wasn't found out, he wasn't run to ground. It
wasn't suspicion founded on any knowledge relevant to his
real identity; she knew nothing of the clandestine world of
revolution, when she walked in the streets of the dirty city

among the angry, the poor and the unemployed they had 'nothing to do' with her—she'd said it. Who he was didn't exist for her; he was safe. She could seek only to place him intriguingly within the alternatives she knew of—was there some financial scandal behind his anonymity, was there a marriage he was running away from—these were the calamities of her orbit. Never in her wildest imagination could she divine what he was doing, there in her bed.

And then it struck him that this was not her bed: this time she had not taken him into the bed she shared with the husband. Not in those sheets; ah, he understood this was the sign he knew *he* would divine, when the time came. Clean sheets on that bed, not to be violated. The husband was coming home tomorrow. *Just for tonight.*

He left early. She did not urge him to stay for breakfast on the terrace. He must get back to bath and change . . . She nodded as if she knew what was coming. —Before getting to the site.— She waved to him as to a friend, down there at the gates, for the eyes of the manservant and a gardener who was singing a hymn while mowing the lawn. He had made a decision, in the respite she granted him. He would take a chance of leaving the city and going to a small town where there was an old contact, dropped out of activity long ago, who might be prevailed upon to revive old loyalties and take him in.

It was perhaps a mistake; who knows. Best safety lies in crowds. The town was too small to get lost in. After three days when the old contact reluctantly kept him in an outhouse in the company of a discarded sewing machine, stained mattresses and mouse droppings, he went out for air one early morning in his host's jogging outfit looking exactly like all the other overweight men toiling along the streets, and was soon aware that a car was following. There was nothing to do but keep jogging; at a traffic light the car drew up beside him and two plain-clothes men ordered him to come to the police station with them. He had a fake document with him, which he presented with the indignation of a good citizen, but at the station they had a dossier that established his identity. He was taken into custody and escorted back to Johannesburg, where he was detained in prison. He was produced at the trial for which he had been the missing accused and the press published photographs of him from their files. With and without a beard; close-cropped and curly-headed; the voracious, confident smile was the constant in these personae. His successful evasion of the police for many months made a sensational story certain to bring grudging admiration even from his enemies.

In his cell, he wondered—an aside from his preoccupation with the trial, and the exhilaration, after all, of being once again with his comrades, the fellow accused—he wondered whether she had recognized him. But it was unlikely she would follow reports of political trials. Come to think of it, there were no newspapers to be seen around her house, that house where she thought herself safe among trees, safe from the threat of him and his kind, safe from the present.

What Were You Dreaming?

I'm standing here by the road long time, yesterday, day before, today. Not the same road but it's the same—hot, hot like today. When they turn off where they're going, I must get out again, wait again. Some of them they just pretend there's nobody there, they don't want to see nobody. Even go a bit faster, *ja*. Then they past, and I'm waiting. I combed my hair; I don't want to look like a *skollie*. Don't smile because they think you being too friendly, you think you good as them. They go and they go. Some's got the baby's napkin hanging over the back window to keep out this sun. Some's not going on holiday with their kids but is alone; all alone in a big car. But they'll never stop, the whites, if they alone. Never. Because these *skollies* and that kind've spoilt it all for us, sticking a gun in the driver's neck, stealing his money, beating him up and taking the car. Even killing him. So it's buggered up for us. No white wants some guy sitting behind his head. And the blacks—

when they stop for you, they ask for money. They want you must pay, like for a taxi! The blacks!

But then these whites: they stopping; I'm surprised, because it's only two—empty in the back—and the car it's a beautiful one. The windows are that special glass, you can't see in if you outside, but the woman has hers down and she's calling me over with her finger. She ask me where I'm going and I say the next place because they don't like to have you for too far, so she say get in and lean into the back to move along her stuff that's on the back seat to make room. Then she say, lock the door, just push that button down, we don't want you to fall out, and it's like she's joking with someone she know. The man driving smiles over his shoulder and say something—I can't hear it very well, it's the way he talk English. So anyway I say what's all right to say, yes master, thank you master, I'm going to Warmbad. He ask again, but man, I don't get it—*Ekskuus*? Please? And she chips in—she's a lady with grey hair and he's a young chap—My friend's from England, he's asking if you've been waiting a long time for a lift. So I tell them— A long time? Madam! And because they white, I tell them about the blacks, how when they stop they ask you to pay. This time I understand what the young man's saying, he say, And most whites don't stop? And I'm careful what I say, I tell them about the blacks, how too many people spoil it for us, they robbing and killing, you can't blame white people. Then he ask where I'm from. And she laugh and look round where I'm behind her. I see she know I'm from the Cape, although she ask me. I tell her I'm from the Cape Flats and she say she suppose I'm not born there, though, and she's right, I'm born in Wynberg, right there in Cape Town. So she say, And they moved you out?

Then I catch on what kind of white she is; so I tell her, yes, the government kicked us out from our place, and she say to the young man, You see?

He want to know why I'm not in the place in the Cape Flats, why I'm so far away here. I tell them I'm working in Pietersburg. And he keep on, why? Why? What's my job, everything, and if I don't understand the way he speak, she chips in again all the time and ask me for him. So I tell him, panel beater. And I tell him, the pay is very low in the Cape. And then I begin to tell them lots of things, some things is real and some things I just think of, things that are going to make them like me, maybe they'll take me all the way there to Pietersburg.

I tell them I'm six days on the road. I not going to say I'm sick as well, I been home because I was sick—because *she's* not from overseas, I suss that, she know that old story. I tell them I had to take leave because my mother's got trouble with my brothers and sisters, we seven in the family and no father. And s'true's God, it seem like what I'm saying. When do you ever see him except he's drunk. And my brother is trouble, trouble, he hangs around with bad people and my other brother doesn't help my mother. And that's no lie, neither, how can he help when he's doing time; but they don't need to know that, they only get scared I'm the same kind like him, if I tell about him, assault and intent to do bodily harm. The sisters are in school and my mother's only got the pension. *Ja.* I'm working there in Pietersburg and every week, madam, I swear to you, I send my pay for my mother and sisters. So then he say, Why get off here? Don't you want us to take you to Pietersburg? And she say, of course, they going that way.

And I tell them some more. They listening to me so nice,

and I'm talking, talking. I talk about the government, because I hear she keep saying to him, telling about this law
and that law. I say how it's not fair we had to leave Wynberg
and go to the Flats. I tell her we got sicknesses—she say
what kind, is it unhealthy there? And I don't have to think
what, I just say it's *bad, bad,* and she say to the man, *As I
told you.* I tell about the house we had in Wynberg, but it's
not my grannie's old house where we was all living together
so long, the house I'm telling them about is more the kind
of house they'll know, they wouldn't like to go away from,
with a tiled bathroom, electric stove, everything. I tell them
we spend three thousand rands fixing up that house—my
uncle give us the money, that's how we got it. He give us
his savings, three thousand rands. (I don't know why I say
three; old Uncle Jimmy never have three or two or one in
his life. I just say it.) And then we just kicked out. And
panel beaters getting low pay there; it's better in Pietersburg.

He say, but I'm far from my home? And I tell her again,
because she's white but she's a woman too, with that grey
hair she's got grown-up kids—Madam, I send my pay home
every week, s'true's God, so's they can eat, there in the
Flats. I'm saying, *six days on the road.* While I'm saying it,
I'm thinking; then I say, look at me, I got only these clothes,
I sold my things on the way, to have something to eat. *Six
days on the road.* He's from overseas and she isn't one of
those who say you're a liar, doesn't trust you—right away
when I got in the car, I notice she doesn't take her stuff
over to the front like they usually do in case you pinch
something of theirs. Six days on the road, and am I tired,
tired! When I get to Pietersburg I must try borrow me a
rand to get a taxi there to where I live. He say, Where do

you live? Not in town? And she laugh, because he don't know nothing about this place, where whites live and where we must go—but I know they both thinking and I know what they thinking; I know I'm going to get something when I get out, don't need to worry about that. They feeling bad about me, now. Bad. Anyhow it's God's truth that I'm tired, tired, that's true.

They've put up her window and he's pushed a few buttons, now it's like in a supermarket, cool air blowing, and the windows like sunglasses: that sun can't get me here.

The Englishman glances over his shoulder as he drives.
'Taking a nap.'
'I'm sure it's needed.'
All through the trip he stops for everyone he sees at the roadside. Some are not hitching at all, never expecting to be given a lift anywhere, just walking in the heat outside with an empty plastic can to be filled with water or paraffin or whatever it is they buy in some country store, or standing at some point between departure and destination, small children and bundles linked on either side, baby on back. She hasn't said anything to him. He would only misunderstand if she explained why one doesn't give lifts in this country; and if she pointed out that in spite of this, she doesn't mind him breaking the sensible if unfortunate rule, he might misunderstand that, as well—think she was boasting of her disregard for personal safety weighed in the balance against decent concern for fellow beings.

He persists in making polite conversation with these passengers because he doesn't want to be patronizing; picking them up like so many objects and dropping them off again, silent, smelling of smoke from open cooking fires, sun and sweat, there behind his head. They don't understand his Englishman's English and if he gets an answer at all it's a deaf man's guess at what's called for. Some grin with pleasure and embarrass him by showing it the way they've been taught is acceptable, invoking him as *baas* and *master* when they get out and give thanks. But although he doesn't know it, being too much concerned with those names thrust into his hands like whips whose purpose is repugnant to him, has nothing to do with him, she knows each time that there is a moment of annealment in the air-conditioned hired car belonging to nobody—a moment like that on a no-man's-land bridge in which an accord between warring countries is signed—when there is no calling of names, and all belong in each other's presence. He doesn't feel it because he has no wounds, neither has inflicted, nor will inflict any.

This one standing at the roadside with his transistor radio in a plastic bag was actually thumbing a lift like a townee; his expectation marked him out. And when her companion to whom she was showing the country inevitably pulled up, she read the face at the roadside immediately: the lively, cajoling, performer's eyes, the salmon-pinkish cheeks and nostrils, and as he jogged over smiling, the unselfconscious gap of gum between the canines.

A sleeper is always absent; although present, there on the back seat.

'The way he spoke about black people, wasn't it surprising? I mean—he's black himself.'

'Oh no he's not. Couldn't you see the difference? He's a Cape Coloured. From the way he speaks English—couldn't you hear he's not like the Africans you've talked to?'

But of course he hasn't seen, hasn't heard: the fellow is dark enough, to those who don't know the signs by which you're classified, and the melodramatic, long-vowelled English is as difficult to follow if more fluent than the terse, halting responses of blacker people.

'Would he have a white grandmother or even a white father, then?'

She gives him another of the little history lessons she has been supplying along the way. The Malay slaves brought by the Dutch East India Company to their supply station, on the route to India, at the Cape in the seventeenth century; the Khoikhoi who were the indigenous inhabitants of that part of Africa; add Dutch, French, English, German settlers whose back-yard progeniture with these and other blacks began a people who are all the people in the country mingled in one bloodstream. But encounters along the road teach him more than her history lessons, or the political analyses in which they share the same ideological approach although he does not share responsibility for the experience to which the ideology is being applied. She has explained Acts, Proclamations, Amendments. The Group Areas Act, Resettlement Act, Orderly Movement and Settlement of Black Persons Act. She has translated these statute-book euphemisms: people as movable goods. People packed onto trucks along with their stoves and beds while front-end loaders scoop away their homes into rubble. People dumped somewhere else. Always somewhere else. People as the figures, decimal points and multiplying zero-zero-zeros into which individual lives—Black Persons Orderly-Moved, -Effluxed, -Grouped—coagulate and compute. Now he has here in the car the intimate weary odour of a young man to whom these things happen.

'Half his family sick . . . it must be pretty unhealthy, where they've been made to go.'

She smiles. 'Well, I'm not too sure about that. I had the

feeling, some of what he said . . . they're theatrical by nature. You must take it with a pinch of salt.'

'You mean about the mother and sisters and so on?'

She's still smiling, she doesn't answer.

'But he couldn't have made up about taking a job so far from home—and the business of sending his wages to his mother? That too?'

He glances at her.

Beside him, she's withdrawn as the other one, sleeping behind him. While he turns his attention back to the road, she is looking at him secretly, as if somewhere in his blue eyes registering the approaching road but fixed on the black faces he is trying to read, somewhere in the lie of his inflamed hand and arm that on their travels have been plunged in the sun as if in boiling water, there is the place through which the worm he needs to be infected with can find a way into him, so that he may host it and become its survivor, himself surviving through being fed on. Become like her. Complicity is the only understanding.

'Oh it's true, it's all true . . . not in the way he's told about it. Truer than the way he told it. All these things happen to them. And other things. Worse. But why burden us? Why try to explain to us? Things so far from what we know, how will they ever explain? How will we react? Stop our ears? Or cover our faces? Open the door and throw him out? They don't know. But sick mothers and brothers gone to the bad—these are the staples of misery, mmh? Think of the function of charity in the class struggles in your own country in the nineteenth century; it's all there in your literature. The lord-of-the-manor's compassionate daughter carrying hot soup to the dying cottager on her father's estate. The 'advanced' upper-class woman comforting her cook when the honest drudge's daughter takes to whoring for a living. *Shame*, we say here. Shame. You must've heard it? We think it means, what a pity; we think we are expressing sympathy—for them. *Shame*. I don't know what we're saying about ourselves.' She laughs.

'So you think it would at least be true that his family were kicked out of their home, sent away?'

'Why would anyone of them need to make that up? It's an everyday affair.'

'What kind of place would they get, where they were moved?'

'Depends. A tent, to begin with. And maybe basic materials to build themselves a shack. Perhaps a one-room prefab. Always a tin toilet set down in the veld, if nothing else. Some industrialist must be making a fortune out of government contracts for those toilets. You build your new life round that toilet. His people are Coloured, so it could be they were sent where there were houses of some sort already built for them; Coloureds usually get something a bit better than blacks are given.'

'And the house would be more or less as good as the one they had? People as poor as that—and they'd spent what must seem a fortune to them, fixing it up.'

'I don't know what kind of house they had. We're not talking about slum clearance, my dear; we're talking about destroying communities because they're black, and white people want to build houses or factories for whites where blacks live. I told you. We're talking about loading up trucks and carting black people out of sight of whites.'

'And even where he's come to work—Pietersburg, whatever-it's-called—he doesn't live in the town.'

'Out of sight.' She has lost the thought for a moment,

watching to make sure the car takes the correct turning. 'Out of sight. Like those mothers and grannies and brothers and sisters far away on the Cape Flats.'

'I don't think it's possible he actually sends all his pay. I mean how would one eat?'

'Maybe what's left doesn't buy anything he really wants.'

Not a sound, not a sigh in sleep behind them. They can go on talking about him as he always has been discussed, there and yet not there.

Her companion is alert to the risk of gullibility. He verifies the facts, smiling, just as he converts, mentally, into pounds and pence any sum spent in foreign coinage. 'He didn't sell the radio. When he said he'd sold all his things on the road, he forgot about that.'

'When did he say he'd last eaten?'

'Yesterday. He said.'

She repeats what she has just been told: 'Yesterday.' She is looking through the glass that takes the shine of heat off the landscape passing as yesterday passed, time measured by the ticking second hand of moving trees, rows of crops, country-store stoeps, filling stations, spiny crook'd fingers of giant euphorbia. Only the figures by the roadside waiting, standing still.

Personal remarks can't offend someone dead-beat in the back. 'How d'you think such a young man comes to be without front teeth?'

She giggles whisperingly and keeps her voice low, anyway. 'Well, you may not believe me if I tell you...'

'Seems odd...I suppose he can't afford to have them replaced.'

'It's—how shall I say—a sexual preference. Most usually you see it in their young girls, though. They have their front teeth pulled when they're about seventeen.'

She feels his uncertainty, his not wanting to let comprehension lead him to a conclusion embarrassing to an older woman. For her part, she is wondering whether he won't find it distasteful if—at her de-sexed age—she should come out with it: for cock-sucking. 'No one thinks the gap spoils a girl's looks, apparently. It's simply a sign she knows how to please. Same significance between men, I suppose . . . A form of beauty. So everyone says. We've always been given to understand that's the reason.'

'Maybe it's just another sexual myth. There are so many.'

She's in agreement. 'Black girls. Chinese girls. Jewish girls.'

'And black men?'

'Oh my goodness, you bet. But we white ladies don't talk about that, we only dream, you know! Or have nightmares.'

They're laughing. When they are quiet, she flexes her shoulders against the seat-back and settles again. The streets of a town are flickering their text across her eyes. 'He might have had a car accident. They might have been knocked out in a fight.'

They have to wake him because they don't know where he wants to be set down. He is staring at her lined white face (turned to him, calling him gently), stunned for a moment at this evidence that he cannot be anywhere he ought to be; and now he blinks and smiles his empty smile caught on either side by a canine tooth, and gulps and gives himself a shake like someone coming out of water. 'Sorry! Sorry! Sorry madam!'

What about, she says, and the young man glances quickly, his blue eyes coming round over his shoulder: 'Had a good snooze?'

'Ooh I was finished, master, finished, God bless you for the rest you give me. And with an empty stummick, you know, you dreaming so real. I was dreaming, dreaming, I didn't know nothing about I'm in the car!'

It comes from the driver's seat with the voice (a real Englishman's, from overseas) of one who is hoping to hear something that will explain everything. 'What were you dreaming?'

But there is only hissing, spluttery laughter between the two white pointed teeth. The words gambol. 'Ag, nothing, master, nothing, all *non*-sunce—'

The sense is that if pressed, he will produce for them a dream he didn't dream, a dream put together from bloated images on billboards, discarded calendars picked up, scraps of newspapers blown about—but they interrupt, they're asking where he'd like to get off.

'No, anywhere. Here it's all right. Fine. Just there by the corner. I must go look for someone who'll praps give me a rand for the taxi, because I can't walk so far, I haven't eaten nothing since yesterday . . . just here, the master can please stop just here—'

The traffic light is red, anyway, and the car is in the lane nearest the kerb. Her thin, speckled white arm with a skilled flexible hand, but no muscle with which to carry a load of washing or lift a hoe, feels back to release the lock he is fumbling at. 'Up, up, pull it up.' She has done it for him. 'Can't you take a bus?'

'There's no buses Sunday, madam, this place is ve-ery bad for us for transport, I must tell you, we can't get nowhere Sundays, only work-days.' He is out, the plastic bag with the radio under his arm, his feet in their stained, multi-striped jogging sneakers drawn neatly together like those of a child awaiting dismissal. 'Thank you madam, thank you master, God bless you for what you done.'

The confident dextrous hand is moving quickly down in the straw bag bought from a local market somewhere along the route. She brings up a pale blue note (the Englishman recognizes the two-rand denomination of this currency that he has memorized by colour) and turns to pass it, a surreptitious message, through the open door behind her. *Goodbye master madam*. The note disappears delicately as a tit-bit finger-fed. He closes the door, he's keeping up the patter, *goodbye master, goodbye madam*, and she instructs— 'No, bang it. Harder. That's it.' *Goodbye master, goodbye madam*—but they don't look back at him now, they don't have to see him thinking he must keep waving, keep smiling, in case they should look back.

She is the guide and mentor; she's the one who knows the country. She's the one—she knows that too—who is accountable. She must be the first to speak again. 'At least if he's hungry he'll be able to buy a bun or something. And the bars are closed on Sunday.'

Keeping Fit

Breathe.

Breath. A baby, a chicken hatching—the first imperative is to breathe.

Breathless.

Breathe! Out of this concentration, in which he forgets even the rhythm of his feet, is a bellows pumped by the command, the admonition, the slap on the bottom that shocks the baby into inhalation—comes his second wind. Unless you go out like this, morning and evening, you never know what no one can remember, that first discovery of independent life: I can breathe.

It came after twenty minutes or so, when he had left behind houses he had never entered but knew because they were occupied by people like himself, passed the aggressive monitoring of dogs who were at their customary gateposts, the shuttered take-away, *prego rolls & jumbo burgers*, and the bristling security cage of the electricity sub-station. These were his pedometer: three kilometres. Here where the grid of his familiar streets came up short against the main road was the point of no return. Sometimes he took a circuitous route back but this was the outward limit. Not quite a highway, the road divided the territory of Alicewood, named for the daughter of a real estate developer, from Enterprise Park, the landscaped industrial buffer between the suburb and the black township whose identity was long overwhelmed by a squatter camp which had spread to the boundary of the industries and, where there was vacant ground, dragged through these interstices its detritus of tin and sacking, abutting on the highway. Someone—the municipality—had put up a high corrugated metal fence to shield passing traffic from the sight.

At six o'clock on a Sunday morning the four-lane road is deserted. A wavering of smoke from last night's cooking fires hangs peacefully, away on the other side, the sign of existence there. In the house he has left, a woman, three children, sleep on unaware that he has risen from her bed, passed their doors, as if he has left his body in its shape impressed beside her and moved out of himself on silent running shoes. The exhausted tarmac gives off a bitumen scent that is lost in carbon monoxide fumes during the week; he is quietly attracted, at his turning point, to mark time a few paces out on the road, having the pounded surface all to himself. It is pleasant as a worn rubber mat underfoot.

He began to run steadily along it. Now no landmarks of distance; instead, memory in a twin stream started to flow in its own progression, the pumping of his heart sending blood to open up where in his brain cells flashes of feeling and images from boyhood were stored at one with the play of fragments from the past week. Tadpoles wriggling in his pocket on his way home from school and the expression of irritation round his accountant's mouth when he disputed some calculation, the change in the curve of a girl's buttocks as she shifted her weight from one leg to another standing in front of him in a bank queue on Friday and the sudden surfacing of his father's figure bending about in a vegetable garden, looming, seen at the height of a child who has done wrong (run away, was it?); the same figure and not the same, with an arthritic leg laid out like a wooden one and the abstracted glance of someone able now only to move towards death, the scent of the girl in the bank as her sharp exhalation of impatience sent the message of her body to his—all this smoothly breathed, in and out. In the flowing together of contexts the crow of a cock in the city does not come incongruously but is more of a heraldic announcement: day, today, time for ghosts to fade, time to return. The cock-crow sounds from over there behind the fence, a place which itself has come about defying context, plan, definition, confusing the peasant's farmyard awakening with the labourer's clock-in at the industries close by.

Of course, they kept chickens among whatever dirt and degradation was behind that fence. He must have done another couple of kilometres; there were no more factory buildings but the shanties occupied the land all along the other side of the road. Here in places the metal fence had collapsed under the pressure of shelters that leant against it and sections had been filched to roof other shacks, yet the life in there was not exposed to the road because the jumbled crowding of makeshift board and planks, bits of wrecked vehicles, cardboard and plastic sheeting closed off from view how far back the swarm of habitation extended. But as he turned to go home—it burst open, revealing itself.

Men came flying at him. The assault exaggerated their faces like close-ups in film; for a vivid second he saw rather than felt through the rictus of his mouth and cheek muscles the instant gaping fear that must have opened his mouth and stretched his cheeks like a rubber mask. They rushed over him colliding with him, swerving against him, battering him. But in their passage: they were carrying him along with them. They were not after him. Fuses were blowing in the panic impulses along the paths of his brain, he received incoherently the realization that he was something in their path—a box they tripped over, an abandoned tyre-tube bowling as they kicked past it—swept into their pursuit. What had seemed to be one of them was the man they were after, and that man's terror and their rage were a single fury in which he hadn't distinguished one from the other. The man's shirt was ripped down the back, another hobbled wildly with one shoe lost, some wore red rags tied pirate-style round their heads, knobbed clubs swung above them, long pieces of wire strong and sharp enough to skewer a man armed them, one loped with a sledge-hammer over his shoulder, there were cleavers, and a butcher's knife ground to sword-point and dangling from a bracelet of plaited red plastic. They were bellowing in a language he didn't need to understand in order to understand, the stink of adrenaline sweat was coming from the furnace within them. The victim's knees pumped up almost to his chin, he zigzagged about the road, the road that was never to be crossed, and the tight mob raced with him, hampered and terrible with their weaponry, and he who had blundered into the chase was whirled along as if caught up by some carnival crowd in which, this time, the presence of death was not fancy dress.

The race of pursued and pursuers broke suddenly from

one side of the road to the other, he was thrust to the edge
of the wild press and saw his chance.

Out.

The fence was down. The squatter shacks: he was on the
wrong side. The road was no longer the sure boundary
between that place and his suburb. It was the barrier that
prevented him from getting away from the wrong side. In
the empty road (*would no one come, would no one stop it*)
the man went down under chants and the blows of a club
with a gnarled knob as big as a child's head, the butcher's
knife plunged, the pointed wires dug, the body writhed
away like a chopped worm. On the oil stains of the tarmac
blood was superimposing another spill.

He fled down among the shacks. Two bare-arsed children
squatting to pee jumped up and bounded from him like
rats. A man lifted the sack over an aperture in tin and
quickly let it fall. There were cooking pots and ashes and
a tethered donkey, the scabby body of a car like the evis-
cerated shell of a giant beetle, lamed supermarket trolleys,
mud walls, beer cans; silence. Desertion; or the vacuum
created by people left behind by the passage of violence,
keeping out of it, holding breath. The haphazard strips of
muddy passage between whatever passed for walls were so
narrow he seemed to have entered a single habitation
where, unseen, people all around followed him—his
breathing, his panting breath—from room to room. A white
man! He felt himself only to be a white man, no other
identity, no other way to be known: to pull aside a sack and
say, I'm in brokerage, give his name, his bona fide address—
that was nothing, these qualifications of his existence meant
nothing. And then a woman appeared out of a shack that
had a door. —Get inside. It's dangerous.— A firm grip, a
big butterscotch-coloured upper arm in a tight-filled short

sleeve, yellow- and pink-flowered. He ducked into her doorway with a push from her in his back.

—They terrible, those people, they'll kill anybody. They will.— She had the strict face formed by respectability, a black woman churchgoer's face, her eyes distant and narrowed behind butterfly-shaped spectacle frames with gilt scrolls. Other people in dimness were staring. A piece of canvas hung over what must be a square of window. Light came only from the gaps between tin walls and the roof low on his head. —You see, I run . . . I was just on the other side of the road, out for a run . . .—

A young man who was turned away from this apparition, paring his nails, children, a stooping man in pyjama trousers and a pullover, a girl with a blanket wrapped round her body below naked shoulders, *doek* awry from sleep.

He had a momentary loss of control, wanting to collapse against the woman, clutch her used big body under her apron and take the shield of her warmth against his trembling. —What's happening—who was it—he's dead there, in the road.—

She spoke for everyone. —From the hostel. They come from the hostel, they come in here and kill us.—

—I read about it.— His head wagged like a puppet's, down, down to his chest.

—You read about it!— She gave a short slap of a laugh. —Every night, we don't know. They come or they don't come—

—Who are they?—

—The police send them.—

He could not say to this woman, That's not what I read.

—Tomorrow it can be *him*.— The woman uncrossed her fine arms and presented the profile of the young man.

—Him?—

—Yes, my son. Come and knock on the wall shouting it's all right, call him comrade so he'll believe, and if he doesn't go out, break in and beat my husband, there, you see him, he's an old man already—take my son and kill him.—

Nothing moves a man on behalf of others so surely as danger to himself. —It was wonderful of you to open your door like that. I mean, for me. I don't know what to say. Why him? What would make them come for your son?—

The young man shifted abruptly, turning still more pointedly away from the apparition his mother had brought in among them.

—My son's in the Youth—the street committee.—

The kind who burned government appointees' houses, stoned buses, boycotted schools. And lived here—slowly he was making out of the dimness and his own shock what this habitation was. Its intimacy pressed around him, a mould in which his own dimensions were redefined. He took up space where the space allowed each resident must be scrupulously confined and observed. The space itself was divided in two by curtains which stretched across it, not quite drawn closed, so that he could see the double bed with a flounced green satin cover which filled one half. A table with pots and a spirit stove, a dresser with crockery, a sagging armchair into which the old man sank, a chromium-shiny radio cassette player, a girlie calendar, Good Shepherd Jesus, framed, with a gold tinsel halo, the droop of clothes hanging from nails, vague darkness of folded blankets—that was the second half. He saw now there were three children as well as the grown daughter and son; seven people lived here.

The woman had lit the spirit stove and she gave an order,

in their language, to the girl. Holding the blanket in one hand and shuffling with her knees together in modesty, the girl fetched a cup and saucer from the dresser, wiped them with a rag, put a spoon of powdered milk in the cup and, chivvied again by her mother, a spoon of tea in a jug. Like a sleep-walker. No one spoke except the woman. But he felt their awareness of him: the old man bewildered as at a visitor he hadn't been told to expect, the children in unblinking curiosity, the young man hostile, the girl—the girl wanting to sink through the earth that was the shack's floor; as if *he* were the threat, and not the marauders whose gales of anger blew about from the road, rising and fading as a wind would gust against the tin walls. The old man suddenly got up and signalled him to take the armchair.

—Please—stay where you are, I don't need—

The woman brought him the cup of tea, carrying a small tin of sugar. —No, no, sit, sit. You see what this place is like, the rain pours in, you see how we have to try and stuff around the tin with plastic, but we can still greet with a chair.—

While he drank the paraffin-tasting tea she stood above him admonishingly. —You must keep away from here.—

—I don't usually come so far, it was just only this morning, and I was right on the other side of the main road, there was no one . . . it happened, I got in the way.—

She pinched her lips between her teeth and shook her head at foolishness. —What do you want to come near this place for.—

Don't take any chances keep away from the main road— his wife, when he ran sometimes before going to bed at night, possessive, not wanting him to do anything that excluded her.

—I can rather go to my home there in Lebowa, but how can we go, he's got a job in town, he's the attendant at underground parking, you'll see him there by the chain where the cars come in to go down under the building. He's too old to stay here now alone.—

The baying from the road swerved away out of hearing. Morning sounds, of coughing, wailing babies, and the drumming of water on tin containers, were released. He stood up and put the cup down carefully on the table.

—Wait.— She turned and said something to the young man. He answered with the smouldering obstinacy of adolescence. She spoke once more, and he put his head out of the door. All held the exact position in which the narrow stream of morning sunlight found them; the boy slipped out and closed them into dimness behind him. The woman did not speak while he was away. Darkness danced with the after-vision of the boy's profile against glare; the waiting was the first atmosphere shared with the one to whom refuge had been given. He could hear them breathing as he breathed.

The son came back surly and said nothing. His mother went up to challenge him face to face. And he answered in monosyllables she drew from him.

—It's all right now. But you like to run, so run.— He felt she was teasing him, in the relief of tension. But she would not presume to laugh with a white man, her matronly dignity was remote as ever.

He shook hands with the old man, thanking him, thanking them all, awkwardly, effusively—no response, as he included the children, the son and daughter—hearing his own voice as if he were talking to himself.

He opened the door. With crossed arms, she contemplated him. —God bless you.—

The telling of it welled up in his mouth like saliva; he was on the right side, running home to tell what had happened to him. He swallowed and swallowed in urgency, unable to get there fast enough. Now and then his head tossed as he ran; in disbelief. All so quick. A good pace, quiet and even on the soft tarmac, not a soul in sight, and before you have the time to take breath—to prepare, to decide what to do—it happens. Suddenly, this was sensational. That's how it will happen, always happens everywhere! Keep away. They came over, at him, not after him, no, but making him join them. At first he didn't know it, but he was racing with them after blood, after the one who was to lie dying in the road. That's what it really means to be caught up, not to know what you are doing, not to be able to stop, say no!—that awful unimagined state that has been with you all the time. And he had nothing to give the woman, the old man; when he ran, he kept on him only a few silver coins along with his house key in the minute pocket which, like the cushioned pump action of their soles, was a feature of his shoes. Could hardly tip her coins. But if he went back, another time, with say, a hundred rands, fifty rands, would he ever find the shack among so many? Should have asked her where she worked, obviously she must be a domestic or something like that, so that he could have rewarded her properly, found her at her place of employment. Where was it the husband held one of those chains you see before the ramp of a firm's underground car park? Had she named the street? How shit-scared he must have been (he jeered) not to take in properly what the woman said! She probably saved his life; he felt the euphoria of survival. It lasted through the pacing of half a block. A car with men in golf caps, going to tee off early, passed him, and several joggers, just up, approached and went by with a comradely lift of the hand; he felt that his experience must blaze in his face if only they had known how to look, if only they had learnt.

But don't exaggerate.

Had his life really been in danger? He could have been killed by a blow to get him out of the way, yes, that sledgehammer—it might have struck a glancing blow. The butcher's knife, cleaver, whatever the horrible thing was with its sword-point and that woven bracelet like the pretty mats they make and sell on the streets, it could scalp you, open your throat with one swing. But they didn't even seem to see him. They saw only the one they were after, and it wasn't him. Under the rise and fall of his feet on the grassy suburban pavement blood drew its pattern on tarmac.

Who knew whether she was telling the truth when she said it was the police who sent them to make trouble?

He read the papers, for all he knew it could have been Inkatha murdering someone from the ANC, it could have been people from the street committees she said the boy belonged to, out to get a local councillor regarded as a government stooge, it could have been ANC people avenging themselves on a police informer. He didn't know how to read the signs of their particular cause as someone like her would from the rags they had tied round their heads or the kind of weapons they'd improvised for themselves, the cries they chanted. He had to believe her, whatever she'd chosen to tell him. Whatever side she was on—god knows,

did she know herself, shut in that hovel, trying to stay alive—
she had opened her door and taken him in.

Why?

Why should she have?

God bless you.

Out of Christian caritas? Love—that variety? But he was
not welcome in the hovel, she had kept the distaste, the
resentment, the unease at his invasion at bay, but herself
had little time for his foolish blundering. *What do you want
to come near this place for.* He heard something else: *Is there
nowhere you think you can't go, does even this rubbish dump
belong to you if you need to come hiding here, saving your
skin.* And he had shamefully wanted to fling himself upon
her, safe, safe, reassured, hidden from the sound and sight
of blows and blood as he could be only by one who belonged
to the people who produced the murderers and was not a
murderer.

As he came level with the security cage of the electricity
sub-station, the take-away, and then the garage and the
houses prefiguring his own, the need to tell began to subside
inside him with the slowing of his heartbeat. He heard
himself describing his amazement, his shock, even (disarm-
ingly honest confession) his shit-scaredness, enjoying the
tears (dread of loss) in the eyes of his wife, recounting the
humble goodness of the unknown woman who had put out
her round butterscotch-coloured arm and pulled him from
danger, heard himself describing the crowded deprivation
of the shack where too few possessions were too many for
it to hold, the bed curtained for some attempt at the altar
of privacy; the piously sentimental conclusion of the bless-
ing, as he was restored to come home for breakfast. The
urge to tell buried itself where no one could get it out of

him because he would never understand how to tell; how to get it all straight.

—A bit excessive, isn't it? Exhausting yourself— His wife was half-reproachful, half-amused at the sight of shining runnels on his face and his mouth parted the better to breathe. But she was trailing her dressing-gown, barefoot, only just out of bed and she certainly had no idea how early he had left or how long he had been absent while the house slept. Over her cereal his daughter was murmuring to a paper doll in one of the imaginary exchanges of childhood, he could hear the boys racing about in the garden; each day without fingerprints, for them.

He drank a glass of juice, and another, of water. —I'll eat later.—

—I should think so! Go and lie down for a while. Are you trying to give yourself a heart attack? What kind of marathon is this. How far have you been today, anyway?—

—I don't keep track.—

—Yes, that's evident, my darling! You don't.—

In the bedroom the exercise bicycle, going nowhere.

In brokerage, her darling, resident at this address. He took off his running shoes and threw his shirt on the carpet. He stank of the same sweat as those he was caught up among within a pursuit he did not understand.

The unmade bed was blissful. Her lilac-patterned blue silk curtains were still drawn shut but the windows were open and the cloth undulated with a breeze that touched his moist breast-hair with a light hand. He closed his eyes. Some extremely faint, high-pitched, minute sound made timid entry at the edge of darkness; he rubbed his ear, but it did not cease. Longing to sleep, he tried to let the sound sink away into the tide of his blood, his breath. If he opened his eyes and was distracted by the impressions of the room— the dressing-table with the painted porcelain hand where her necklaces and ear-rings hung, the open wardrobe with his ties dangling thick on a rack, a red rose tripled in the angle of mirrors, his briefcase abandoned for the weekend on the chaise-longue, the exercise bicycle—he heard the sound only by straining to. But the moment he was in darkness it was there again: plaintive, feeble, finger-nail scratch of sound. He staggered up and went slowly about the room in search of the source like a blind man relying on one sense alone. It was behind a wall somewhere, penetrating the closed space of his head from some other closed space. A bird. A trapped bird. He narrowed the source; the cheeping came from a drain-pipe outside the window.

His bare feet slapping flat-footed with fatigue, he slumped back to the breakfast table. —There's a bird trapped in the drain-pipe outside the bedroom.—

—So the kids told me.—

—Well let them take the ladder and get it out.—

—It must be a chick from the nest those mynahs built under the eaves. Fell into the gutter and then down the pipe, so it's stuck—what can the boys do?—

—So what's to be done about it?—

—Can't exactly call the fire brigade. Poor little thing. Just wait for it to die.—

Back in the room, on the bed, he listened. Eyes closed. Every time the sound paused he had to wait for it to begin again. Die. It would not die. In another darkness the most insignificant of fragments of life cried out, kept crying out. He jumped from the bed and burst through the house, going after her, bellowing, his hands palsied with rage. —Get the bloody thing out, can't you! Push up a pole, take the ladder, pull down the drain-pipe, for Christ' sake!—

She stared at him, distancing herself from this exhibition.

—What do you expect of little boys? I won't have them break their necks. Do it then! *You* do it. Do it if you can. You're so athletic.—

Amnesty

When we heard he was released I ran all over the farm and through the fence to our people on the next farm to tell everybody. I only saw afterwards I'd torn my dress on the barbed wire, and there was a scratch, with blood, on my shoulder.

He went away from this place nine years ago, signed up to work in town with what they call a construction company—building glass walls up to the sky. For the first two years he came home for the weekend once a month and two weeks at Christmas; that was when he asked my father for me. And he began to pay. He and I thought that in three years he would have paid enough for us to get married. But then he started wearing that T-shirt, he told us he'd joined the union, he told us about the strike, how he was one of the men who went to talk to the bosses because some others had been laid off after the strike. He's always been good at talking, even in English—he was the best at the farm school, he used to read the newspapers the Indian wraps soap and sugar in when you buy at the store.

There was trouble at the hostel where he had a bed, and riots over paying rent in the townships and he told me— just me, not the old ones—that wherever people were fighting against the way we are treated they were doing it for all of us, on the farms as well as the towns, and the unions were with them, he was with them, making speeches, marching. The third year, we heard he was in prison. Instead of getting married. We didn't know where to find him, until he went on trial. The case was heard in a town far away. I couldn't go often to the court because by that time I had passed my Standard 8 and I was working in the farm school. Also my parents were short of money. Two of my brothers who had gone away to work in town didn't send home; I suppose they lived with girl-friends and had to buy things for them. My father and other brother work here for the Boer and the pay is very small, we have two goats, a few cows we're allowed to graze, and a patch of land where my mother can grow vegetables. No cash from that.

When I saw him in the court he looked beautiful in a blue suit with a striped shirt and brown tie. All the accused—his comrades, he said—were well-dressed. The union bought the clothes so that the judge and the prosecutor would know they weren't dealing with stupid *yes-baas* black men who didn't know their rights. These things and everything else about the court and trial he explained to me when I was allowed to visit him in jail. Our little girl was born while the trial went on and when I brought the baby to court the first time to show him, his comrades hugged him and then hugged me across the barrier of the prisoners' dock and they had clubbed together to give me some money as a present for the baby. He chose the name for her, Inkululeko.

Then the trial was over and he got six years. He was sent to the Island. We all knew about the Island. Our leaders had been there so long. But I have never seen the sea except to colour it in blue at school, and I couldn't imagine a piece of earth surrounded by it. I could only think of a cake of dung, dropped by the cattle, floating in a pool of rain-water they'd crossed, the water showing the sky like a looking-glass, blue. I was ashamed only to think that. He had told me how the glass walls showed the pavement trees and the other buildings in the street and the colours of the cars and the clouds as the crane lifted him on a platform higher and higher through the sky to work at the top of a building.

He was allowed one letter a month. It was my letter because his parents didn't know how to write. I used to go to them where they worked on another farm to ask what message they wanted to send. The mother always cried and put her hands on her head and said nothing, and the old man, who preached to us in the veld every Sunday, said tell my son we are praying, God will make everything all right for him. Once he wrote back, That's the trouble—our people on the farms, they're told God will decide what's good for them so that they won't find the force to do anything to change their lives.

After two years had passed, we—his parents and I—had saved up enough money to go to Cape Town to visit him. We went by train and slept on the floor at the station and asked the way, next day, to the ferry. People were kind; they all knew that if you wanted the ferry it was because you had somebody of yours on the Island.

And there it was—there was the sea. It was green *and* blue, climbing and falling, bursting white, all the way to the sky. A terrible wind was slapping it this way and that; it hid the Island, but people like us, also waiting for the ferry, pointed where the Island must be, far out in the sea that I never thought would be like it really was.

There were other boats, and ships as big as buildings that go to other places, all over the world, but the ferry is only for the Island, it doesn't go anywhere else in the world, only to the Island. So everybody waiting there was waiting for the Island, there could be no mistake we were not in the right place. We had sweets and biscuits, trousers and a warm coat for him (a woman standing with us said we wouldn't be allowed to give him the clothes) and I wasn't wearing, any more, the old beret pulled down over my head that farm girls wear, I had bought relaxer cream from the man who comes round the farms selling things out of a box on his bicycle, and my hair was combed up thick under a flowered scarf that didn't cover the gold-coloured rings in my ears. His mother had her blanket tied round her waist over her dress, a farm woman, but I looked just as good as any of the other girls there. When the ferry was ready to take us, we stood all pressed together and quiet like the cattle waiting to be let through a gate. One man kept looking round with his chin moving up and down, he was counting, he must have been afraid there were too many to get on and he didn't want to be left behind. We all moved up to the policeman in charge and everyone ahead of us went onto the boat. But when our turn came and he put out his hand for something, I didn't know what.

We didn't have a permit. We didn't know that before you come to Cape Town, before you come to the ferry for the Island, you have to have a police permit to visit a prisoner on the Island. I tried to ask him nicely. The wind blew the voice out of my mouth.

We were turned away. We saw the ferry rock, bumping the landing where we stood, moving, lifted and dropped by all that water, getting smaller and smaller until we didn't know if we were really seeing it or one of the birds that looked black, dipping up and down, out there.

The only good thing was one of the other people took the sweets and biscuits for him. He wrote and said he got them. But it wasn't a good letter. Of course not. He was cross with me; I should have found out, I should have known about the permit. He was right—I bought the train tickets, I asked where to go for the ferry, I should have known about the permit. I have passed Standard 8. There was an advice office to go to in town, the churches ran it, he wrote. But the farm is so far from town, we on the farms don't know about these things. It was as he said; our ignorance is the way we are kept down, this ignorance must go.

We took the train back and we never went to the Island— never saw him in the three more years he was there. Not once. We couldn't find the money for the train. His father died and I had to help his mother from my pay. For our people the worry is always money, I wrote. When will we ever have money? Then he sent such a good letter. That's what I'm on the Island for, far away from you, I'm here so that one day our people will have the things they need, land, food, the end of ignorance. There was something else—I could just read the word 'power' the prison had blacked out. All his letters were not just for me; the prison officer read them before I could.

He was coming home after only five years!

That's what it seemed to me, when I heard—the five years were suddenly disappeared—nothing!—there was no whole year still to wait. I showed my—our—little girl his photo again. That's your daddy, he's coming, you're going to see him. She told the other children at school, I've got a daddy, just as she showed off about the kid goat she had at home.

We wanted him to come at once, and at the same time we wanted time to prepare. His mother lived with one of his uncles; now that his father was dead there was no house of his father for him to take me to as soon as we married. If there had been time, my father would have cut poles, my mother and I would have baked bricks, cut thatch, and built a house for him and me and the child.

We were not sure what day he would arrive. We only heard on my radio his name and the names of some others who were released. Then at the Indian's store I noticed the newspaper, *The Nation*, written by black people, and on the front a picture of a lot of people dancing and waving—I saw at once it was at that ferry. Some men were being carried on other men's shoulders. I couldn't see which one was him. We were waiting. The ferry had brought him from the Island but we remembered Cape Town is a long way from us. Then he did come. On a Saturday, no school, so I was working with my mother, hoeing and weeding round the pumpkins and mealies, my hair, that I meant to keep nice, tied in an old *doek*. A combi came over the veld and his comrades had brought him. I wanted to run away and wash but he stood there stretching his legs, calling, hey! hey! with his comrades making a noise around him, and my mother started shrieking in the old style aie! aie! and my father was clapping and stamping towards him. He held his arms open to us, this big man in town clothes, polished shoes, and all the time while he hugged me I was holding my dirty hands, full of mud, away from him behind his back. His teeth hit me hard through his lips, he grabbed at my mother and she struggled to hold the child up to him. I thought we would all fall down! Then everyone was quiet. The child hid behind my mother. He picked her up but she turned her head away to her shoulder. He spoke to her gently but she wouldn't speak to him. She's nearly six years old! I told her not to be a baby. She said, That's not him.

The comrades all laughed, we laughed, she ran off and he said, She has to have time to get used to me.

He has put on weight, yes; a lot. You couldn't believe it. He used to be so thin his feet looked too big for him. I used to feel his bones but now—that night—when he lay on me he was so heavy, I didn't remember it was like that. Such a long time. It's strange to get stronger in prison; I thought he wouldn't have enough to eat and would come out weak. Everyone said, Look at him!—he's a man, now. He laughed and banged his fist on his chest, told them how the comrades exercised in their cells, he would run three miles a day, stepping up and down on one place on the floor of that small cell where he was kept. After we were together at night we used to whisper a long time but now I can feel he's thinking of some things I don't know and I can't worry him with talk. Also I don't know what to say. To ask him what it was like, five years shut away there; or to tell him something about school or about the child. What else has happened, here? Nothing. Just waiting. Sometimes in the daytime I do try to tell him what it was like for me, here at home on the farm, five years. He listens, he's interested, just like he's interested when people from the other farms come to visit and talk to him about little things that happened to them while he was away all that time on the Island. He smiles and nods, asks a couple of questions and then stands up and stretches. I see it's to show them it's enough, his mind is going back to something he was busy with before they came. And we farm people are very slow; we tell things slowly, he used to, too.

He hasn't signed on for another job. But he can't stay at home with us; we thought, after five years over there in the middle of that green and blue sea, so far, he would rest with us a little while. The combi or some car comes to fetch him and he says don't worry, I don't know what day I'll be back. At first I asked, what week, next week? He tried to explain to me: in the Movement it's not like it was in the union, where you do your work every day and after that you are busy with meetings; in the Movement you never know where you will have to go and what is going to come up next. And the same with money. In the Movement, it's not like a job, with regular pay—I know that, he doesn't have to tell me—it's like it was going to the Island, you do it for all our people who suffer because we haven't got money, we haven't got land—look, he said, speaking of my parents', my home, the home that has been waiting for him, with his child: look at this place where the white man owns the ground and lets you squat in mud and tin huts here only as long as you work for him—*Baba* and your brother planting his crops and looking after his cattle, Mama cleaning his house and you in the school without even having the chance to train properly as a teacher. The farmer owns us, he says.

I've been thinking we haven't got a home because there wasn't time to build a house before he came from the Island; but we haven't got a home at all. Now I've understood that.

I'm not stupid. When the comrades come to this place in the combi to talk to him here I don't go away with my mother after we've brought them tea or (if she's made it for the weekend) beer. They like her beer, they talk about our culture and there's one of them who makes a point of putting his arm around my mother, calling her the mama of all of them, the mama of Africa. Sometimes they please her very much by telling her how they used to sing on the Island and getting her to sing an old song we all know from our grandmothers. Then they join in with their strong voices. My father doesn't like this noise travelling across the veld; he's afraid that if the Boer finds out my man is a political, from the Island, and he's holding meetings on the Boer's land, he'll tell my father to go, and take his family with him. But my brother says if the Boer asks anything just tell him it's a prayer meeting. Then the singing is over; my mother knows she must go away into the house.

I stay, and listen. He forgets I'm there when he's talking and arguing about something I can see is important, more important than anything we could ever have to say to each other when we're alone. But now and then, when one of the other comrades is speaking I see him look at me for a moment the way I will look up at one of my favourite children in school to encourage the child to understand. The men don't speak to me and I don't speak. One of the things they talk about is organizing the people on the farms—the workers, like my father and brother, and like his parents used to be. I learn what all these things are: minimum wage, limitation of working hours, the right to strike, annual leave, accident compensation, pensions, sick and even maternity leave. I am pregnant, at last I have another child inside me, but that's women's business. When they talk about the Big Man, the Old Men, I know who these are: our leaders are also back from prison. I told him about the child coming;

he said, And this one belongs to a new country, he'll build the freedom we've fought for! I know he wants to get married but there's no time for that at present. There was hardly time for him to make the child. He comes to me just like he comes here to eat a meal or put on clean clothes. Then he picks up the little girl and swings her round and there!—it's done, he's getting into the combi, he's already turning to his comrade that face of his that knows only what's inside his head, those eyes that move quickly as if he's chasing something you can't see. The little girl hasn't had time to get used to this man. But I know she'll be proud of him, one day!

How can you tell that to a child six years old. But I tell her about the Big Man and the Old Men, our leaders, so she'll know that her father was with them on the Island, this man is a great man, too.

On Saturday, no school and I plant and weed with my mother, she sings but I don't; I think. On Sunday there's no work, only prayer meetings out of the farmer's way under the trees, and beer drinks at the mud and tin huts where the farmers allow us to squat on their land. I go off on my own as I used to do when I was a child, making up games and talking to myself where no one would hear me or look for me. I sit on a warm stone in the late afternoon, high up, and the whole valley is a path between the hills, leading away from my feet. It's the Boer's farm but that's not true, it belongs to nobody. The cattle don't know that anyone says he owns it, the sheep—they are grey stones, and then they become a thick grey snake moving—don't know. Our huts and the old mulberry tree and the little brown mat of earth that my mother dug over yesterday, way down there, and way over there the clump of trees round the chimneys

and the shiny thing that is the TV mast of the farmhouse—
they are nothing, on the back of this earth. It could twitch
them away like a dog does a fly.

I am up with the clouds. The sun behind me is changing
the colours of the sky and the clouds are changing themselves, slowly, slowly. Some are pink, some are white, swelling like bubbles. Underneath is a bar of grey, not enough
to make rain. It gets longer and darker, it grows a thin snout
and long body and then the end of it is a tail. There's a
huge grey rat moving across the sky, eating the sky.

The child remembered the photo; she said *That's not him*.
I'm sitting here where I came often when he was on the
Island. I came to get away from the others, to wait by myself.

I'm watching the rat, it's losing itself, its shape, eating
the sky, and I'm waiting. Waiting for him to come back.

Waiting.

I'm waiting to come back home.

FOR THE BEST IN PAPERBACKS, LOOK FOR THE 🐧

In every corner of the world, on every subject under the sun, Penguin represents quality and variety – the very best in publishing today.

For complete information about books available from Penguin – including Puffins, Penguin Classics and Arkana – and how to order them, write to us at the appropriate address below. Please note that for copyright reasons the selection of books varies from country to country.

In the United Kingdom: Please write to *Dept JC, Penguin Books Ltd, FREEPOST, West Drayton, Middlesex, UB7 0BR.*

If you have any difficulty in obtaining a title, please send your order with the correct money, plus ten per cent for postage and packaging, to *PO Box No 11, West Drayton, Middlesex*

In the United States: Please write to *Dept BA, Penguin, 299 Murray Hill Parkway, East Rutherford, New Jersey 07073*

In Canada: Please write to *Penguin Books Canada Ltd, 2801 John Street, Markham, Ontario L3R 1B4*

In Australia: Please write to the *Marketing Department, Penguin Books Australia Ltd, P.O. Box 257, Ringwood, Victoria 3134*

In New Zealand: Please write to the *Marketing Department, Penguin Books (NZ) Ltd, Private Bag, Takapuna, Auckland 9*

In India: Please write to *Penguin Overseas Ltd, 706 Eros Apartments, 56 Nehru Place, New Delhi, 110019*

In the Netherlands: Please write to *Penguin Books Netherlands B.V., Postbus 3507, NL–1001 AH, Amsterdam*

In West Germany: Please write to *Penguin Books Ltd, Friedrichstrasse 10–12, D–6000 Frankfurt/Main 1*

In Spain: Please write to *Alhambra Longman S.A., Fernandez de la Hoz 9, E–28010 Madrid*

In Italy: Please write to *Penguin Italia s.r.l., Via Como 4, I-20096 Pioltello (Milano)*

In France: Please write to *Penguin France S.A., 17 rue Lejeune, F-31000 Toulouse*

In Japan: Please write to *Longman Penguin Japan Co Ltd, Yamaguchi Building, 2–12–9 Kanda Jimbocho, Chiyoda-Ku, Tokyo 101*

A Guest of Honour

Evelyn Bray has returned to a newly created African State and accepted the temporary post of special education adviser. In doing so he falls into the trap of 'nice white liberals getting mixed up in things they don't understand'. Or was it infinitely more complicated than that?

'*A Guest of Honour*, Nadine Gordimer's massive book about an ex-colonial Englishman's affair with a new African State, is a novel of total immersion – physical, moral, social, political. It teems with human life, with landscapes of the map and of the mind, with events and insights – a deeply impressive work' – *Guardian*

Winner of the James Tait Black Memorial Prize

The Late Bourgeois World

One Saturday morning Liz Van den Sandt opens a telegram which tells her that her ex-husband, Max, has drowned himself.

Much had drowned with him. They had wanted to live *well*, in the best, most honourable sense: not at the cost of others – something not possible in South Africa when you were white. And Max, highly strung, sensitive and intelligent, found it increasingly impossible to bear the burden of betrayal and the slow erosion of his self-respect.

'Superb' – *The New York Times*

BY THE SAME AUTHOR

The Conservationist

'A triumph of style . . . this is a novel of enormous power' – Paul Theroux in the *New Statesman*

Mehring is rich. He has all that white privilege in South Africa can give him. Isolated, at once cold and passionate, he challenges history in his determination that nothing shall change his way of life.

'One of those rare works of literature that command special respect for artistic daring and fulfilled ambition' – Paul Bailey in the *Observer*

Something Out There

This powerful collection of short stories and a novella reflects Nadine Gordimer's extraordinary ability to illuminate the connection between the personal and the political in the divided society of South Africa. With compassion and scrupulous honesty Gordimer penetrates to the core of the human heart, revealing the subtlest feelings of her characters – black and white, revolutionaries and racists, adulterers, spinsters and lovers.

'One of the major artistic achievements of our time' – Elizabeth Hardwick in the *New York Review of Books*

A Sport of Nature

'A spontaneous, pretty white girl, disturbing to men and most alive in her own sexuality, is transformed into a political activist, intent on returning the whole African continent to the rule of Africans ... This is the bold theme of Nadine Gordimer's new novel ... an exhilarating book' – *Observer*

'Apartheid is the narrow, metallic counter on which Gordimer throws down her human coinage to test its essential trueness ... she writes with an energy and beauty as remarkable as that of her heroine' – *Spectator*

July's People

It is war. For years the situation has been 'deteriorating'. Now all over South Africa the cities are battlegrounds. Bam and Maureen Smales – enlightened, liberal whites – are rescued from the terror by their servant, July, who leads them to refuge in his native village.

What happens to the Smales, and to July, mirrors the changes in the world – and gives us glimpses into a chasm of hatred and misunderstanding.